SLEEP MODE

DAN HOLT

MaxHoltMedia

CONTENTS

Prologue

A small gleaming Craft descended into the clearing deep in the woods behind the farmhouse of David and Jewel Krebs. After putting a lean surefooted earth creature to sleep, the Alien Visitor began an electronic sweep of the animal's biological system.

Suddenly, from the concealment of the trees a smaller creature, projecting painfully penetrating sounds, came charging at him. The Visitor rushed into his ship, secured the entrance behind him, and accelerated into the sky.

Upon reaching safety the Visitor logged the event, unaware that he had dropped one of the small devices that he used to induce the Sleep Mode in biological specimens.

Chapter 1

REPEAT

"Hurry Steven, it's a three-hour drive to your grandmother's house and we have to be back here by four o'clock to make our flight."

"Okay, Mom," Steven answered from his room then looked up at his dad standing in the hall. "Has Grandpa and Grandma got the Internet yet?" he asked hopefully.

Steven's dad put his hand on his shoulder. "No, and I don't think they are going to. They are in their seventies and happy and content just like they are. Most of their lives were spent before the internet and the fast-changing world of computers. You can take your laptop with you and some of your computer games. However, you might just find that these two weeks could be quite an adventure. Repeat's there and lots of trails that I made some twenty-five or so years ago. Try walking them again."

Steven worked his laptop and collection of game CD's into his suitcase. His computer games were a part of his world here in the city that he could take to the country to have something to do during the two weeks at Grandma's house.

Steven, twelve, five-foot-four, skinny, brown eyes, black hair, loved his Grandpa and Grandma. They were okay but Grandpa was always playing dominoes with a bunch of other grandpas at the feed store and Grandma was always sewing clothes to sell at the Show and Sell section of a store over on the highway. With his laptop he could survive the two weeks in the country until Mom and Dad picked him up to return to the city. And, Steven thought, he and Repeat, Grandpa's dog, could explore and stuff.

"Get the rest of your things into the car, Steven," Donald Krebs said to his son, "we have to leave right away."

Steven picked up his two suitcases and started for the car. As he exited the door he heard his father call his grandparents on the phone.

"It'll be good to see Repeat again," he muttered.

The car slowed. Steven looked up when his father turned off the highway onto the sandy road that went the last five hundred yards and into Grandma's front yard. David and Jewel Krebs, Grandpa and Grandma, were standing on the front porch when they drove into the yard and up under the large oak tree.

Beside the house was Grandma's vine arbor. Its frame was completely covered with honeysuckle vines. Steven saw a hummingbird darting from blossom to blossom. Then his eyes went to the flock of chickens in the back yard. They were randomly pecking the ground, walking about, jerking their heads forward as they walked, and pecking the ground again. He heard the random clucking. To the right was a fresh water well with a pump house next to it. Beyond that was the corral and inside was the barn. A cow was drinking from the watering trough. The large animal raised her head and looked when the car stopped. Water was dripping from her mouth.

Grandma's House

Steven jumped out of the car and headed over to the big oak tree to look for his initials, carved there by himself last summer. Finding them, he leaned over for a closer look. They were further down the tree. He could have sworn that he had carved them higher up on the tree than that. *"Maybe the tree settles lower in the ground as it grows and gets heavier,"* he thought.

"You've grown, Stevie," Grandpa said. Steven looked up at his grandfather; he was smiling. "Hi, Grandpa," Steven said and hugged him.

"Stevie, you're getting so big," Grandma said. "I'm so glad you have come to visit with us. Repeat has missed you," she added as she hugged him.

Repeat, Grandpa's dog, wagging his tail from mid-torso on back, barked his unusually loud, penetrating bark. So loud that everyone stopped and looked down at him. Repeat, glanced at Grandpa, and barked a much softer bark. Grandpa nodded; he had had a few talks with Repeat about that bark on behalf of the cows and chickens.

Repeat, named by Grandpa Krebs, had come up to the farmhouse years ago as a stray looking for food. Grandpa tossed him a soup bone with left-over meat on it. Repeat grabbed the bone and retreated into the woods for a feast. Later, he returned for more. A 'repeat,' Grandpa had called it. He gave the dog that name and Repeat had been there ever since.

While his parents and grandparents were talking, Steven reached down to pet Repeat on the head. Repeat barked again, raised up on his hind legs, and put his paws on Steven's waist. "Hello, Repeat," Steven said, rolling the canine's head between his hands.

Steven's Mom and Dad hugged Steven and said their goodbye's to Grandpa and Grandma, with promises of calling regularly to check on Steven, then drove away on the sandy road and on to the airport to tend to the business waiting in Paris. Steven picked up his two suitcases and took them to the spare room and began unpacking. His mind began to replay some of the memories from last summer.

Chapter 2

THE DEVICE

Steven was awakened by the sun's rays falling on the antique dresser on the far side of the bedroom. He raised up on his elbow and looked around. Grandma's house. He was at Grandma's house. He heard the birds singing; probably very happy that the tree frogs and crickets, that sang their chorus through the night, had finally shut up. Steven dressed and went into the kitchen. Grandma was turning the bacon. "Where's Grandpa?"

"Good morning, Stevie. Did you sleep okay?"

"Yes, Grandma."

"Your grandpa's out in the barn milking the cows." Steven headed out the door. As he was walking across the corral his grandfather came out of the barn carrying two pales of milk.

"Good morning, Grandpa," Steven said.

"Stevie, you're up already, how are you doing this morning?"

"Fine."

"Good," his grandpa said, "here, carry this bucket for me." Steven took the gallon bucket two-thirds full of thick milk. Grandpa was carrying a two-gallon bucket when they started for the house. Steven paused a moment and looked down toward the creek that ran across the farm just beyond the corral and down the hill. His eyes found the walk bridge he built last summer. It was a thick wooden plank laid across the creek with a stake driven at each end to keep it in place. He thought he saw a *crawdad* duck under the water. *"I'll have to go down and check out my bridge,"* he thought.

After breakfast Grandpa went into the living room and picked up the morning paper as he did every morning. Leafing through it a second page headline caught his eye:

UFO spotted over Red River County. Eye witnesses claim they saw a silvery ball fly over Red River and disappear to the north.

Grandpa smiled to himself, folded the paper and laid it on the couch then left for the feed store and his domino games.

Steven left the breakfast table and headed for the front door. Repeat hopped up, ready for an adventure. Steven walked around the end of the porch and into the vine arbor; Repeat followed. He looked at the wooden bench at the back wall of vines, then up at the ceiling at the vines hanging down in several places. The honeysuckle smelled good. In the back corner of vine arbor Steven saw a hummingbird dart about two feet to another blossom. He was surprised at how fast the tiny bird could fly.

"Repeat, humming birds are really fast." Repeat barked a mild agreement. Steven petted Repeat on the head.

Steven, alone and in charge, walked out of the vine arbor, across the yard, down the hill, and across 'his' bridge. The creek was four feet wide, three inches deep, with very clear flowing water. Steven put his hand in the stream; it was cold just as he remembered. He saw crawdad 'chimneys' scattered along the creek bank. They looked like tiny versions of the rock chimneys back home in the park where people barbecued on weekends. They were made of balls of mud the size of marbles. The outside of the little chimneys was dried; the inside, still wet. Steven picked up one; a suddenly-exposed crawdad ran sideways to the water, then shot backwards out of sight. Repeat jumped at the creature, stopping short when his nose touched the water. He shook the water off his nose and barked.

"Repeat," Steven said, "crawdads swim backward. They can't see where they are going, only where they've been. Of course, they can tell if their pursuer is gaining on them.

Maybe that's why they swim backward." He smiled, stood and looked up and down the creek again. "Come on, Repeat."

Steven began following the creek downstream, occasionally tossing a stick or a rock into the water. He came to a fence surrounding the farm, crawled through, and continued on. He stopped and picked up a stick three feet long and then continued walking the trail, swatting weeds and grass along the way. The creek was wider here and the water was flowing much slower. He saw a dragonfly land on top of the water. The insect was slowly moving downstream with the flowing creek. Steven wondered why it didn't sink into the water. Maybe he had tiny balloons in his feet. The insect rose from the water and sped away. He looked around and started downstream again.

The woods became thick. Steven continued to follow the trail made by the feet of an earlier explorer. As his adventure continued he noticed that the trail was overgrown with grass and weeds in places. His dad wasn't here now to keep them worn away. He was grown up and in the city where there's lots of noise and stuff. He's too old to explore anyway. He already knows everything.

Repeat suddenly turned toward the deep woods and barked, loud. Too loud.

"What is it?" Steven said. Repeat barked again, loudly, then, looking up at Steven, barked a much softer bark. He then looked back in the direction of the deep woods. Steven took a few steps in that direction. Repeat barked again and started running into the deep woods.

"Repeat!" Steven yelled at the dog. Repeat stopped and sat down and whined. Steven walked up and patted him on the head. "What is it, boy?"

Repeat whined and looked in the direction again.

"Okay, we'll go look but walk with me, don't run," Steven said, shaking his finger at the dog. Repeat cocked his head to the side and whined.

As Steven started into the woods Repeat walked beside him looking up at him and then into the woods. Repeat would occasionally venture ahead, look around, pause and wait for Steven, then go on.

"I don't see anything," Steven said a few minutes later and stopped. Repeat walked up twenty feet ahead, sat down, and waited. Steven followed.

After half an hour of ducking under low hanging branches and making their way around dense undergrowth they came upon an oblong clearing. It was a spot in the woods with no trees, just thick bushes and clumps of grass. Steven stood at the edge of the clearing and looked around. Right out in the middle there was a deer feeder. It was a barrel with three legs bolted to it that held it two feet above the ground. It had a pan mounted on the bottom of the barrel. Steven went up to it and looked in the pan. It was filled with a mixture of animal feed. He picked up some of the mixture between his thumb and finger and looked at it, dropped it back in the pan, dusted his fingers, and wiped them on his shirt.

Repeat barked at the feeder barrel and looked at Steven. Steven walked around the barrel, studying it, wondering why it was there. He saw some deer tracks next to the it. He squatted down and examined them, placing his finger down into one, then following them with his eyes. The tracks led into the thick woods.

A gentle breeze ruffled Steven's hair. Repeat looked upwind and sniffed the air. He barked that loud penetrating bark and ran several feet in that direction, then stopped, sat down, and whined.

The canine's limited mental faculties reconstructed the event associated with the odd scent in the breeze. Repeat had been here before. He had been hidden in the trees watching an odd smelling Creature look at a deer that was lying on the ground. Repeat had barked, loud. The Creature ran for his ship: Repeat charged him barking rapidly. The Creature ran through a doorway. The door suddenly appeared right in front of Repeat— closed! His nose took the full impact of bringing his body to a stop. And, as if that wasn't enough, his own tail slapped him on top of the head.

Repeat whined again. Still a dog with a dog's instincts, Repeat barked and ran toward the scent, stopping at a bush and barking at it, circling around and around it.

"Repeat, come back here!" Steven yelled at the dog. Repeat ignored the instructions and kept barking at the bush. Steven cautiously eased up behind him and studied the bush. "What is it, boy, something in that bush?"

Repeat looked up at Steven then back at the bush and barked again. Steven glanced around and spotted a stick about two feet long. He picked it up, eased up behind Repeat, held his breath, and tossed it on the bush. Repeat crouched his front legs, ready to pounce.

Nothing.

Steven took a breath then picked up the stick and stuck it into the bush. Still nothing. Repeat stuck his nose into the thick bush as far as he could for a fresh 'reading.' *Still there.* He barked several times, circling the bush again. Steven, braver now, approached the bush, squat down, stuck both hands into it and pushed the thick small branches apart.

Lying down in the bottom of the bush was a dark gray metallic device, three inches long, one-inch wide, and a quarter inch thick. On one end of it was a round glass window the size of a quarter. Just below that there was a button the size of a dime. Steven leaned forward and looked at it closely. Repeat looked at Steven, barked quietly, then looked at the device and whined. Steven reached slowly down into the bush and picked it up.

A green light came on in the round glass window!

Surprised, Steven dropped it. The light went off. Repeat raised his ears and barked twice, watching the device. Steven watched it for a few moments. It was just lying there.

"Repeat, what could it be?" he said. Steven took a breath then again reached down in the bush and picked up the device. The green light came on. He instinctively held it further from himself but kept it in his hand. Nothing happened, just the round green light. He shook it; the light stayed on. Becoming comfortable with it, Steven turned and started walking back toward the deer feeder, watching the green light. Suddenly it turned to a vertical bar. Steven stopped and looked up. Several birds flew away from their feast at the deer feeder. The light turned back round.

"Repeat," Steven exclaimed, "maybe this thing is a bird finder and a bird watcher lost..." as he turned toward Repeat the green light became a vertical bar again. He looked up at Repeat, then back down at the vertical bar of light. He moved the device to one side; the light turned back round, then he aimed it back at Repeat; instantly, the green light was a vertical bar.

"Repeat, maybe this thing finds all hidden things in the woods! Neat!" He held the device straight out with his arm, pushed the button, and did a complete circle.

Steven slowly became aware of the absence of sound.

Dead quiet.

Absolute silence.

Steven heard himself breathing. He looked down at the dog; Repeat's whine was barely audible. Steven looked at the device in his hand and listened; still nothing; just quiet. He didn't know why; he held the device straight out with his arm again, pushed the button, and did the same circle.

All the sounds came back! Repeat barked twice. Steven was overwhelmed. He looked around and spotted a log at the edge of the clearing. He made his way over to it and sat down to think. Repeat sensed his unusual disposition, laid down beside him, and stayed quiet.

Chapter 3

POWER

Steven sat on the log for some time, deep in thought, turning the device over and over in his hands. He looked down at Repeat. "Repeat, a scientist made this. He made it to study the birds and the animals. That way, he wouldn't have to shoot them with tranquilizer darts or anything. He could just put them to sleep, study them for a while, then wake them up and just let them fly away."

Repeat raised his ears and cocked his head to the side as he watched Steven examine the device.

"That way," Steven added, "the scientist wouldn't hurt the animals or anything." Steven was quiet again for a few moments. He looked at the device again, then around at the woods, then at Repeat. "Repeat, suppose you got a thorn in your paw and it was really hurting; I could put you to sleep..." He pointed the device at Repeat; the round green light turned to a vertical bar. Steven, watching the vertical bar of light, pushed the button; the vertical bar switched to sideways; a horizontal bar.

Repeat collapsed instantly!

Steven, startled by the instant response and the lifeless collapse of his friend, quickly pushed the button again. Repeat hoped up and resumed his position, cocking his head sideways and waiting as before.

"Repeat, you okay!" Steven said. Repeat's ears went straight up with attention and then down again. The animal was apparently unaware that he was sound asleep seconds earlier.

"Repeat, I didn't know it worked so quick. I thought you would lie down and then go to sleep."

Repeat barked quietly and whined.

"Boy, if you're going to put somebody to sleep, you better make sure they are lying down first. As soon as you push the button; they're asleep." Steven petted Repeat on the head and gestured with the device. "This is our secret, Repeat. Whoever lost it didn't come back out here and get it. They probably just made another one."

Steven put the device in his pocket and started back toward the house. Repeat trotted along with him.

Steven felt different. He had something in his pocket that he could make somebody go to sleep anytime he wanted to. He took a deep breath and sighed.

Steven Wayne Krebs now had power!

He began thinking about his new world. No one could push him around anymore. If somebody bigger than him tried, he'd just put them to sleep and walk away. Steven smiled and breathed a little harder as he experienced the new sensation. He was even with everybody, no, stronger than anybody, except the scientist that made it. He probably has another one by now. Steven would have to keep it secret; no one can know that he has it.

Steven came to the fence, crawled through, and continued up the creek. He walked across his bridge then glanced to his left. There was a crawdad backing toward the creek with his pinchers held up in a defensive posture. The backward swimming creature would step sideways a little then continue to back toward the water. Steven smiled, pulled out the device and pointed it at the crustacean and pushed the button. The crawdad collapsed with his tail straight out. Steven squatted down and picked it up and examined it closely.

The body was hard like a rock; the tail fin looked just like the tail of a fish, only it was sideways instead of up and down. He turned it over and looked at the underside; it was white and ribbed. The legs were grouped in a cluster at the body and spread like a spider. He turned the creature back upright and looked at the head. The eyes looked like two bb-gun pellets glued to the head. The 'whiskers' stuck out from the head and were curled at the ends.

Steven put the crawdad back down on the ground, pointed the device and pushed the button again. The crawdad resumed his defensive posture and continued backing toward the creek.

"You may go," Steven said. Upon reaching the water, the crawdad activated that powerful tail and shot away instantly. Steven smiled and put the device back in his pocket.

Chapter 4

THE LECTURE

"Grandma," Steven said during lunch, "do scientist ever come out here and study the birds and animals?"

"I don't know, Stevie," his grandmother answered, "I suppose they do."

"Well, I was just wondering."

"You like science and things like that, don't you, Stevie."

"Yeah, Grandma. Science can do lots of things. When I grow up I want to be a scientist and invent new things."

"Well," his grandmother said in a warm voice, "I know you're real smart. You can be a scientist if you want to. Your grandfather and I are so proud of you."

Steven went to the guest room, took the device out of his pocket and looked at it, gripped it, and pocketed it again. He opened his laptop, turned it on, then put in his CD, Mega-Race, picked his car, then started firing at the bad guys. Watching the animated laser bursts and hearing the sound effects, his mind went back to the device.

"I didn't see a ray when I pushed the button and Repeat fell asleep on the ground," he mumbled. He pointed the device at the wall and then, watching very closely, pushed the button. Nothing. Just the round green light. "Has it quit working!" Steven exclaimed, then grabbed his mouth, held his breath for a few moments, then sighed with relief. Grandma didn't hear him. He put the device back in his pocket, turned off his laptop, and walked out on the front porch where his grandmother has resumed her sewing. "Grandma, I'm going out exploring again with Repeat."

"Okay, Stevie, be careful and don't go too far."

"I won't, Grandma," Steven promised.

Steven walked hurriedly back down to the creek. Repeat trotted along with him. Looking around, he saw a blackbird sitting on a tree branch on the other side of the stream. Steven slowly removed the device from his pocket; the round green light came on instantly. He aimed it at the bird; the round green light turned to a vertical bar. Steven pushed the button; the vertical bar of light immediately switched to horizontal. The bird fell off the limb onto a bed of leaves below. "It still works, Repeat!" Steven said excitedly as he watched his friend run up to the bird and bark. Repeat pushed the sleeping bird with his nose.

"Repeat, leave the bird alone," Steven said. Repeat backed away and sat down. Steven slipped the device back into his pocket, picked up the sleeping bird, and looked at it closely. It was completely limp, but breathing rhythmically. Steven gently laid the bird back down on the bed of leaves, pulled the device out of his pocket, and looked at Repeat.

"Repeat, I didn't have this pointed at anything. That's why it didn't work in the house. It has to be pointed at something before it will work. When the light is round, that means it's not pointed at anything. When the light is a vertical bar, it means that whatever it's pointed at is awake. When you push the button and the light turns sideways, that means that whatever it's pointed at is asleep instantly." Repeat barked his, now practiced, agreement bark.

"Okay," Steven said, looking at the device, "when you pick it up the round green light comes on; that means it's ready. When you point it at something to put to sleep; the round light turns to a vertical bar; that means that whatever the device is pointed at is awake and the device has locked on. When you push the button, whatever it has locked onto is put to sleep instantly. Now, when you point it at the sleeping bird or animal or somebody, the light will be horizontal, meaning that the creature is asleep and the device has locked on. Pushing the button again wakes them up."

Steven pointed the device at the sleeping bird and pushed the button. The blackbird hoped up, a second later, accelerated on wing until out of sight. Steven turned toward Repeat and opened his hands. "Do you understand?"

Repeat did his usual. Steven nodded.

Chapter 5

RESEARCH

Tuesday morning found Steven up early. He quickly dressed and patted the device in his pocket. Today he would do some research. He had to know how far away it would work. He would test it today and find out. He headed for the dining room. When he stepped through the door his grandfather handed him the small milking pail.

"Good morning, Stevie,"

"Morning." The grandfather-grandson team went out the door and headed for the barn and the morning ritual.

"Grandpa," Steven said, "when did you learn to milk a cow?"

"When I was your age. I've been milking these cows all their lives."

"That's why the cow always stand still for you, Grandpa, and moves her leg out of the way so you can milk her."

Grandpa smiled and nodded. "I think she sees my ugly face and just wants me to finish and leave."

Steven glanced at his grandfather. "You're not ugly, Grandpa. Your face is all wrinkled up because you're old." Steven smiled when his grandfather looked at him then back toward the barn and smiled to himself.

"Thank you, Stevie. Your mom and dad tell me that you're real bright in school."

"I make straight 'A's."

"That's good. Perhaps you should work on the social graces a little."

"I take social studies."

"Good...good." Grandpa Krebs sat down on the stool beside the cow. Steven put his hand on the cow's hip bone as explained by his grandfather and pushed gently. The docile animal set her leg back. Steven smiled. He got on his knees beside his grandpa and watched the smooth methodical motions of the experienced hands milking the cow. A fly buzzed around the cow's back; the cow's tail swatted Steven's cheek. Surprised, he sat back on the ground. Grandpa smiled. "Stevie, are you enjoying your visit here?"

"Yes, Grandpa, me and Repeat explore every day. There's lots of trails."

"That's good. Repeat sure perks up when you are here visiting."

"I like Repeat. He's a good dog."

"Yes, he is. Sometimes I wonder where he came from. You know that he just showed up here one day. There seemed to be something special about him so I fed him and he's now part of the family and this farm. No doubt someone simply stopped, probably over on the highway, and put him out. We were lucky that he made his way here."

"He was lucky, too, Grandpa."

Steven, sitting in the guest room, began laying plans for some research with the device. He had to know all about it when he got back home. He had power. He looked at the device and thought about how wonderful his life would be back home. He had to know how far away it would work just in case he wanted to put somebody to sleep from far away. He put the device back in his pocket and went into the living room. "Grandma, I'm going out with Repeat."

"Okay," his grandmother responded. "Have fun and watch your 'P's and 'Q's."

"Huh?" Steven said.

"Be careful."

"Oh, I will, Grandma." Steven made his way down to the creek, across his home-made bridge, and up the hill to the pasture on the other side. He crawled through the fence and looked around. He saw Grandpa's two cows grazing in the tall grass and swatting at the insects with their tails. He pointed the device at the cow that was grazing near the back fence of the small pasture and looked down at the green light. It stayed round. He swung the device around until it was aimed at the cow standing in the middle of the pasture. The light changed to a vertical bar. He returned the aim of the device to the distant cow. "Okay," he said, "the cow by the back fence is too far away, Repeat." Steven held the device on the distant cow and started walking toward her.

After walking twenty yards or so he saw the round green light switch to a vertical. It had locked on and found the cow awake. Steven stopped, marked the ground with his toe, and began pacing toward the cow, counting his steps. When he walked up to the cow, the domestic animal looked up, walked away a few steps, then her large head went back down into the green grass.

"One hundred and fifty steps," Steven said. "Three hundred feet. Long as a football field, Repeat!" He imagined himself sitting in the stands watching a football game. Everybody there would be within range.

Steven sighed and looked around. Glancing up he saw a hawk flying over. There was two small, faster flying, birds chasing it. The smaller birds would swoop in for an attack, pecking the larger fowl, then darting away just to return again and again. Every time one of the attackers would make contact the hawk would change directions a little and make an effort to fly faster. The smaller birds finally broke off the attack and flew back in the direction from which they had come. The hawk flew on in a straight line to get as far away as it could. Steven's pulse was rapid as he watched the larger bird fly into the distance. Breathing with his mouth open, he looked down at the device, gripped it, and looked back in the direction of the fleeing bird. "Now I can stop them," he whispered.

He sighed again and looked toward the house. He walked back to the fence, crawled through, then sat down under a larger tree near the creek bank and leaned up against the tree trunk. Repeat laid down beside him. Steven turned the device over and over in his hands again. He imagined a scientist, in his laboratory, wearing thick glasses, bent over the device with tiny tools in his hands, connecting wires together.

He wondered what it looked like inside. He carefully inspected the gray metal case. There were no cracks, no screws holding it together, just a completely smooth surface. He held the device up next to his eye, the round green light almost touching his eyeball. He starred into the interior for a few moments. He could barely make out some black webbing that looked kind of like a spider web.

Even if he could, he wouldn't take it apart. It might not work when he put it back together. He couldn't take that chance. It had to work when he got back home. It made everything different.

A butterfly fluttered from his left toward the creek. He pointed the device and pushed the button. The beautiful insect became motionless and spiraled slowly to the ground. Still leaning on the tree, he pushed the button again. The fragile insect fluttered away in the warm sunlight.

POWER

Chapter 6

REPEAT'S TRIAL

Wednesday morning when Steven stepped off the front porch Repeat hopped up ready for the day's activities. Steven petted him on the head then looked toward the patch of woods behind the big oak tree at the edge of the yard. "Repeat, today we're going to explore the old syrup mill. Grandma said it was in the woods behind the big oak tree. She said Grandpa used to make syrup a long time ago."

Repeat's bark had started to sound like: 'I agree.' The pair walked to the large oak tree; Steven laid his hand on his initials. "Repeat, I grow faster than trees do, but they live longer."

Agreement. Steven entered the patch of woods behind the oak tree and made his way down a small hill. He came to the overgrown remains of a road. His eyes followed the road to his right; it went around a hill and ended in the sandy yard in front of the house. He followed the road down the hill. It stopped in front of a small shed.

The old structure was just a frame with only one piece of tin left on its roof. It had been an open-air shed mounted on six poles. Inside, under what was left of the roof, there was a rusty pan three feet wide, six feet long, and four inches deep. Inside the pan there were fins three inches tall that ran crossways about eight inches apart. Steven looked closely; the first fin touched on this side of the pan but had a gap on the other side. The next fin was just the opposite, the gap was on this side. The alternating fins went the full length of the pan. At the other end there was a drain hole and a rusted out bucket sitting under it. Steven picked up the bucket. It fell apart. He dropped it and dusted his hands together.

He remembered his dad talking about his grandpa cooking syrup here; right here in this pan. Lying on the ground near the pan was wooden tool shaped like a garden hoe. He picked it up, bumped the dirt off it on one of the poles, and placed it in the pan. It fit exactly between the fins. "You could push the syrup along through the fins with this," he said out loud.

His dad had said that the juice from the sorghum cane flowed down to this pan from the mill up on the next hill. Steven looked around. The trough was gone. He looked up toward the hill; Repeat was sniffing around a rusty old three roller style mill that was lying on the ground. Steven made his way up the hill to the old abandoned mill and studied the site. The three six-inch diameter posts were still sticking up. The frame built on top of them had rotted away and the mill had fallen to the ground. The three rollers that crushed the cane were grooved. Grass and weeds were growing up between them. "The old days were really something, Repeat," Steven said.

Suddenly, Repeat whirled around and started barking. There was a rustling in the weeds and an animal jumped up and started running. Steven pulled out the device, pointed it, and pushed the button. A lean jack rabbit tumbled to a stop. Repeat dove at it.

"Repeat!" Steven yelled, running up behind him. Repeat backed away and started circling the rabbit barking lightly and whining. Steven picked up the jack rabbit by his back legs. Repeat got quiet, sat down, and watched, his ears at attention. The rabbit was three feet long from the tip of his back legs to the tip of his front legs as he hung completely limp in Steven's hand. It was very lean and had ears six inches long. Its flank showed its rhythmic breathing.

The jack rabbit, now in peaceful sleep, was one of few in the East Texas woods. The animal's survival was due to a special gift from nature. The animal had no idea as to what he owed his survival, also he had no idea that he had a serious problem here at this moment.

However, given the opportunity, he would instinctively offer a solution. That gift that nature had given him—speed.

"Repeat, this is a jack rabbit," Steven said. "Grandpa told me about jack rabbits. They are fast, very fast. You couldn't catch him. It takes a greyhound to catch a jack rabbit. Greyhounds are dogs that are a lot bigger than you and a lot faster than you." Repeat kept circling the rabbit and bobbing his head and barking quietly. Steven looked at Repeat, then at the jack rabbit, then back to Repeat. "You want to see if you can catch him?" Repeat barked twice. Steven laid the rabbit down on the grass. "Come here, Repeat." Steven dragged the dog to a spot six feet away from the rabbit.

"Okay, get ready!" Steven leaned forward and pointed the device. Repeat crouched his front legs and laid his chin on the grass; his tail wagged a couple of times.

"You ready!"

Repeat barked. Steven pushed the button. The jack rabbit jumped six feet straight up! Repeat jumped up four feet and fell over backwards on the grass. The excited canine jumped up and whirled around. By the time he got his bearings the jack rabbit had covered sixty feet. Repeat took off after him. By the time he got to the spot, the rabbit had covered another hundred. Repeat quit barking and concentrated on running. Pouring on all he had he got up to thirty miles an hour...the jack rabbit was doing sixty.

Repeat pulled up, trotted a few more yards, then stopped and looked back, then again in the direction in which the swift creature had disappeared. He barked then looked back at Steven.

"I told you," Steven said.

Repeat looked one more time then came walking back to his friend from the city. Steven patted him on the head. "Don't worry about it. You're not a greyhound. Think about this; greyhounds can't bark like you can. Come on, let's go back to the house. I'm thirsty and I'll bet you are, too."

Chapter 7

THE SURPRISE

The morning sun was warm and comfortable as Steven and Repeat made their way down to the creek. The smell of the honeysuckle flourishing on the vine arbor still lingered in Steven's nose. Steven smiled as he watched a scissor-tailed bird open his 'scissors' and glide down and land on a tree branch.

"Repeat," Steven said. "We'll cross the creek, then the pasture, and explore the woods beyond the back fence. Steven walked across his bridge and looked down at the fast moving water. He saw a school of minnows; the small fish, all about two inches long, were swimming against the current, staying in one place momentarily. He pulled out the device, aimed it at the school of creatures swimming in unison and pushed the button. Nothing happened. He aimed the device again and looked at the green light. It stayed round. He swung it over to Repeat; the light turned to a vertical bar.

'Huh,' Steven said. "Repeat, the water is protecting them. The device doesn't work through water. I'll have to remember that. It might not work on somebody if they're wet, or it might not work in the rain."

Repeat, looking at the school of fish, whined, and touched the water with his paw. The minnows scattered in all directions, darting away with amazing speed.

Steven and Repeat made their way from the creek, up the slope, to the fence. Steven stepped through the barbed wire fence. Repeat ducked under, then looked up at Steven. Steven petted Repeat on the head. The pair crossed the pasture, walking past the two cows. The large animals looked around, then their heads went back down into the grass. When the explorers arrived at the back fence, Steven looked up and down it and crawled through, Repeat followed.

There were no trails.

"Repeat, this hasn't been explored very much," Steven said. He noticed that the trees close to the fence were short, about twice his height, then further on the large trees started. He could smell the pine scent, the same as when his mother cleaned at home. He pulled some pine needles off a tree, smelled them and then picked up a pine cone. It was very light, and prickled with pointed 'stickers' on it. He threw it up into one of the large trees. It bounced from limb to limb and fell to the ground. Repeat ran over and smelled it.

Venturing on into the woods, he looked up. A gentle breeze was swaying the tops of the large trees. Last year's leaves were crunching under his feet. A fascinating world unknown in the city. The air was fresh. He could hear birds singing. In the distance he heard: who, who, whooooo. As if an owl was asking a question. He answered: "It's me, Steven and my friend, Repeat."

Steven smiled at himself, looked down at Repeat, and patted him on the head.

The sound of a woodpecker echoed through the woods, sounding like a wooden machine gun. Steven wondered how they could move their heads so fast and peck the tree so hard without popping their eyeballs out of their sockets.

Suddenly, Repeat stopped and barked. Startled, Steven's mind rushed back to the moment. He looked in the direction of his canine friend's interest. Up ahead he could see a big tree, blackened on one side. At the bottom of it there was an opening, almost a perfect triangle. Repeat started running toward the tree and barking.

"Repeat." Steven started running behind him. Repeat got the big tree well ahead of Steven and stuck his nose into the opening. Repeat yelped, whirled around, and started running back toward Steven. The canine shot by Steven at full speed.

"Repeat, where are you going?" Steven yelled toward Repeat.

The scent of the skunk hit Steven's nose.

Steven grabbed his nose and started running after Repeat. Moments later he caught up with him. His friend had his head upside down on the grass. He was walking forward and pushing it like a bull dozer. He then turned his head the other way and rubbed it on the grass some more. He snorted, shook his head, then put his chin on the grass and played bull dozer again. He laid his snout on the grass and rubbed it some more.

"Pheeewwww, Repeat, you stink!" Steven said. Repeat was busy; he was stroking the sides of his snout with his paws.

"Repeat, you stuck your nose right in that hole with that skunk!" Repeat barked; this time it sounded like 'help.'

"Come on, Repeat," Steven said. "I'll take you back to the house and give you a bath." Repeat followed, stopping from time to time to work with his nose. They crossed the pasture, made their way across the creek, then went up to the house. Steven went into the house and up to his grandmother. Grandma Krebs sniffed the air a couple of times and looked at Steven.

"Repeat stuck his nose in a skunk's den," Steven said. "I've got to give him a bath."

"Oh, that poor dog," his grandmother said, getting to her feet. "Go out to the shed; it's in the back. Just inside the door, on the wall, there's a wash tub. Take it to the well and fill it half full of water. There's a garden hose there."

Steven went out the back door, got the tub, hoisted it over his head, and carried it to the well. Repeat was bulldozing the sand in the front yard. Steven set the tub down by the pump house, put the garden hose in it, and turned on the water. A minute later he heard the electric pump inside the pump house start. When the tub was half full he turned off the water. He heard the back door of the house open and looked up. His grandmother came out carrying a large towel over her arm, a bar of soap, and a roasting pan filled with hot water. He could see it steaming. She came to the well, laid the towel and bar of soap down on the grass and poured the hot water into the wash tub. She stirred the water around in the tub with her hand.

"Stevie, give Repeat a bath and I'll lay out a change of clothes for you."

"I didn't get none on me, Grandma," Steven said.

"By the time you give that dog a bath," she said, "you're going to need a change of clothes." Grandma went back into the house.

"Come here, Repeat," Steven said. Repeat looked up, took a few steps toward Steven, then looked at the tub and went over and drank a few laps of water from it. Steven scooped up Repeat and put him in the tub of warm water then reached for the soap. Repeat hopped out of the tub then shook, spraying Steven with water.

"Repeat!" Steven said. Repeat sat down and whined. Steven scooped him up again and put him back in the tub, holding him down in the water. Repeat started splashing the water with his front legs and trying to jump out of the tub again with his back legs. The two bobbed up and down several times, then Steven fell backward with Repeat lying across him. Repeat stood, shook, then hopped off Steven and shook again. Steven sat up, spewed the water out of his mouth, pulled the device out of his pocket, aimed it at Repeat and pushed the button.

Nothing happened. Steven held the device steady and pushed the button again. Still nothing.

"He's too wet," Steven said. "Maybe if I get closer." Steven got up and walked toward Repeat, pushing the button. Repeat backed away. Steven ran at him, pushing the button.

Repeat took off running toward the back yard with Steven in hot pursuit pushing the button. They went across the back yard then around the house. Repeat ran up ahead of Steven and stopped and took the time to shake again. The next time Steven pushed the button Repeat collapsed, sound asleep.

Steven picked up his stinking companion and started back down the side of the house toward the back yard and around to the well. When he reached the back yard, he stopped and stared. His mouth fell open.

The whole back yard was covered with sleeping chickens!

"Oh, no!" Steven said, "I put all Grandma's chickens to sleep!" He glanced at the back door. It was closed. He hurriedly carried Repeat to the well, laid him down on the grass, then ran back to the back yard and started waking up chickens. Every time he pushed the button two or three chickens would jump up and flop their wings. Soon they were all clucking again. Steven ran back to the well.

He picked up Repeat and put him in the tub of water. He soaped his friend good, then sloshed him around in the warm water. When all the soap was washed off he lifted Repeat out of the water and laid him on the grass again. He pulled out the device and pushed the button. Too wet. He reached for the towel, dried Repeat's head, then stuck the device right up in his ear and pushed the button. Repeat hopped up and shook several times then looked at Steven and the tub of water and backed away a few steps.

"Don't worry about it, boy. You've already had a bath and you smell a lot better." Steven dumped the tub of water then hoisted it over his head and started for the shed, then stopped. Lying at the corner of the house was a sleeping chicken. Steven put the tub down, pulled out the device, leveled it over his arm and sighted down it like an expert rifleman, and pushed the button. The chicken jumped up, flopped her wings then ran into the flock.

Chapter 8

THE CARNIVAL

Steven was awake early Saturday morning. He looked out the window at the trees emerging from the darkness as dawn spread across the farm. The tree frogs were concluding their chorus as 'day' invaded the world of nature. Steven's last few days of waking early had added scope to his experience. There was something appealing about it.

"Maybe you don't have to sleep as long when you're in the country," he thought, "there's not at many people breathing the air." He decoded that when he grew up and became a scientist he would have to check that out.

Saturday morning; half way through the two weeks. He was counting the days until he was back in the city, with the device. It sure was going to be different. Since he had found the device, every night he had gone to bed thinking about life after he gets back home. His mind would play out different situations he would get into and how he would use the device. In his imagination he had put the bullies at school to sleep, tied their shoe laces together then awakened them in front of everybody.

At breakfast Steven noticed that Grandpa and Grandma were looking at him and smiling.

"What is it?" he said.

"Stevie, there's a carnival in town this week. Would you like to go?" Grandpa said.

"Yeah!" Steven said excitedly.

"Okay," Grandpa said, "after breakfast we'll drive into town for a little while and you can ride some of the rides. It's nothing like Six Flags Over Texas where you live but folks around here enjoy it when the carnival comes to town."

"It's okay," Steven said. "I think it will be fun."

Grandpa Krebs drove into the make-shift parking lot of the carnival grounds and parked. Steven opened the back door and stepped out of the car. Hearing the carnival music and the chatter of hundreds of voices and the screams of the 'riders' re-oriented him to the hustle and bustle of the city. He loved it. Steven hurried over and got in line for the bumper cars. With only six people in front of him he'd get in on the next run. Small carnivals are neat; you don't have to wait a long time to get on a ride.

As he drove the bumper car around the floor doing head-on and glance-offs with the other young people he noticed the kids were shouting to be heard. Noise! It was great!

As the day wore on Steven rode almost every ride in the carnival. He began to notice the sensation of hunger. He stopped and let his grandparents catch up.

"Grandma, I'm hungry," he said.

"We are too," Grandma said. "Let's go over to the hot dog stand." Steven spotted the hot dog vendor across the grounds and led the way. There was a longer line at the hot dog stand than any of the carnival rides. They got in line and waited, advancing as the people were served. A lady, carrying a large purse, got in line behind them.

Steven saw the running man out of the corner of his eye. He looked around at the stranger. He was bearded, skinny, and had a long pony tail. The man ran by and grabbed the purse from the lady's arm right behind them. The lady screamed and staggered to regain her balance. Steven made a snap decision, pulled out the device, aimed, and pushed the button.

The agile runner was asleep in mid-stride.

He went down on the grass, tumbling to a stop. The purse landed fifteen feet from him. The lady hurried over, picked up her purse, and backed away farther from the sleeping figure. The lady's scream brought the sheriff hurrying across the grounds from the carnival rides.

"Sheriff, that man grabbed my purse", she said, pointing at the man lying on the grass on his side, sleeping soundly. The sheriff looked at the lean bearded man, then at the lady standing there holding her purse with both hands. "What did you do, lady, bean him with it?" There was scattered laughter in the gathering crowd.

"No!" she responded, "he fell." A voice came from the crowd. "Sheriff, he grabbed that lady's purse and was running with it and just went down, like he passed out." The sheriff approached the man, knelt down and placed his fore finger on the man's neck for a moment. Satisfied with the pulse, he looked him over for evidence of an injury. He found none. His breathing was deep and regular.

The sheriff stood up, turned and looked at the crowd, at the lady holding her purse, and then back at the man sleeping on the grass. Steven pushed the button again. The awakened purse snatcher sat up, looked at the crowd, then up at the sheriff and smiled foolishly.

"You okay?" the sheriff said.

"What happened?" the man said in a confused voice, looking around at the crowd.

"You snatched that lady's purse and then fell asleep in a dead run," the sheriff said, smiling. The man looked at the lady, her purse, at his feet and legs, then around at the crowd.

"Maybe you ought to look for another line of work," the sheriff added, "looks like you're a little bored with snatching purses from the ladies. You fell asleep on the job." The crowd roared with laughter. The sheriff smiled broadly. Then he spoke to the man in a serious tone. "Do you want to go to jail, or, do you want to leave town right now?" The man got up and began brushing bits of grass from his clothing. "I'll leave town, Sheriff."

Steven was standing behind his grandparents, breathing with his mouth open; a half smile on his lips. Grandpa Krebs watched the whole thing without saying a word. Steven heard him say softly.

"Darndest think I ever saw."

"It's the times, David," Grandma said, "It's the times."

Steven Krebs felt a new sensation. He was in control of his new power and would always do good with it.

Chapter 9

CHIP AND GYP

"Monday morning," Steven said to himself, "four days, just four more days, and Mom and Dad will be here to pick me up. Then, I'll be home and everything will be different."

During breakfast Steven's grandmother watched as Steven enjoyed his new found taste for biscuits and gravy with bacon. "Stevie, I'm taking several new items to the store today and placing them on the 'Show and Sell' racks.

"I'll help you, Grandma. Can Repeat go with us?"

"That will be okay." Grandma said, smiling at Steven's request.

There was something special about the relationship between a boy and his dog. Repeat was considered to be Steven's dog when Steven was visiting. They spent every day together. Grandma and Grandpa thought it was very special for Steven and were happy that he had welcomed Repeat into his world.

While Grandma was cleaning the kitchen, Steven went out into the front yard. Repeat jumped up with his usual enthusiasm.

"Repeat, we are going to the store with Grandma today." Steven went out to Grandma's car and opened the back door. Repeat jumped up into the car then hopped up on the seat and sat down.

"Repeat, come back out of there; we're going to put the clothes in there." Repeat hopped back out of the car and followed Steven back and forth as he loaded Grandma's newly sewn articles of clothing. Steven closed the car door and went back into the house. Repeat returned to his 'I'll wait here, spot'.

A few minutes later Steven reappeared on the front porch and sat down beside Repeat. He reached over and petted his friend on the head. Repeat's tail thumped the porch.

A half an hour later Grandma appeared in a new dress and hat.

"Grandma, you look good!" Steven said.

"Thank you, Stevie. You ride in the front with me. Put Repeat in the front floorboard of the car." Steven hurried ahead of his grandmother and opened the door of the car for her; then, when she was in and settled, closed it.

"Come on, Repeat." Steven went around to the passenger side and opened the door.

Repeat jumped up into the front seat and sat down. Steven pointed to the floorboard.

"In the floor," he said. Repeat got down in the floorboard of the car, curled up, and laid his chin on his front paws. Steven got in the car, shut the door, and reached down and petted Repeat on the head.

As his grandmother was driving along the blacktopped road toward the country store, Steven noticed that every time he looked down at Repeat the canine would look at Steven and then look away. Steven tried it several times. Each time, Repeat would look at Steven momentarily and look away. They would hold each other's eyes for a moment, then Repeat would look away, then back to Steven's eyes, then away again.

"He knows that I'm smarter that he is," Steven thought, *"and he still likes me."* He reached down and petted Repeat again.

At the country store Steven was busy for a few minutes carrying the clothes inside to his grandmother as she would hang them on the racks in the spacious display area of the store. A whole wall was dedicated to the concept of 'Show and Sell.' The store owner did well with gums, candies, and soft drinks as a result of the people flow brought in by the idea. Steven's grandmother made extra money with the beautiful clothes that came from her skilled hands. Steven looked at the variety of home-sewn shirts hanging on the racks.

"These clothes really look good, Grandma. I wonder if there's a shirt here that will fit me."

"I made two shirts for you, Stevie. They're at home. I'm going to give them to you when you leave Friday to go home."

"Oh, thank you, Grandma."

Steven got a Coke and went outside and sat down on a wooden bench in front of the store. Repeat sat down at the end of it and joined Steven watching the people go in and out of the busy store. Several cars and pickups came and went at the gas pumps. Some would gas up their vehicles, then steer them around to the side of the store and park, then enter the store to shop.

Steven finished his Coke and set the bottle under the bench. When he raised back up a bobtailed truck had pulled up the gas pumps. Riding on the back were two large black dogs. They had stubbed tails and very short ears. Repeat got up on his all fours and raised his ears. Steven glanced at Repeat and then back to the big dogs standing on the truck bed. Both of them had come over to the edge of the truck bed and were looking at Repeat.

One of the larger canines was wearing a black collar with gold buttons braided around it.

The other was wearing a brown collar with silver buttons on it in the same pattern. The owner got out of the truck and started the gas pump fueling the vehicle and then went into the store. When he disappeared inside the two dogs growled at Repeat.

Steven slipped the device out of his pocket and cupped it in his hands. Repeat showed his teeth and growled back at the larger dogs. Steven looked over at Repeat, surprised at how serious he sounded. The large dogs, standing side by side, growled more loudly at Repeat.

Repeat barked that loud penetrating bark. The dog with the brown collar laid his ears back down. The dog with the black collar growled viciously and leaped toward Repeat.

Steven got him in mid-air.

The large dog hit the ground, sound asleep. His twin leaped. Steven pushed the button again just as the brown collared dog landed on his partner. The same influence that put the brown collar to sleep, awakened the sleeping black collar. The startled black collar snapped at the brown collar and wiggled out from under him.

Steven pushed the button again. The black collared canine collapsed on the brown collar's head. The awakened brown collar bit at his twin by instinct. Repeat was adding loud sound effects the whole time.

The dog's owner came running out of the store and pushed his way through the gathering crowd. "Chip, Gyp, what are you doing!" he yelled at his dogs. The dog with the brown collar, Chip, succeeded to authority and jumped back up on the truck bed.

Steven pushed the button one more time. Gyp, with his shiny black collar, jumped up and whirled around a couple of times and barked. Repeat's bark completely drowned him out.

"Get back on that truck," the owner yelled at the dog. Gyp beat a hasty retreat and jumped back upon the truck bed. Steven heard someone in the crowd talking to the owner of the twin dogs.

"Are those trained dogs?"

"No, they're just stupid," was the reply.

Then Steven heard another voice. "That young boy's dog over there sure has a bark on him, don't he?" Steven smiled and petted Repeat on the head. "Way to go, Repeat."

Standing in the background, mingling in the crowd, Merle Finch studied Repeat intently. "Big Bark", he whispered. "That will be his name...Big Bark, I like it."

He waited around until Grandma and Steven, with Repeat, left, and then he went into the store to talk to the owner.

Merle Finch, down on his luck, was laying low for a while. He was on his way to his cousin Buford Thompson's house to hang out until things cooled down. The police were looking for him. He trained dogs for the dog fighting circuit. People betting on the dogs while they were fighting made Merle a lot of money. He was doing fine until the animal rights people raised so much of a stink that the police got involved and were busting people for animal cruelty. They had raided a dog fight where Merle was involved, and got his name, but he managed to slip away and come here to hide out for a while. His cousin, Buford, lived in the deep woods a couple of miles behind the Krebs farm. When Merle Finch saw Repeat take on those two big dogs and stun them with that bark of his, he had to have Repeat for the fighting circuit. He'd never have believed it if he hadn't seen it with his own eyes. That bark of his would make Merle rich.

"You're the owner of this store?" Merle asked. The owner nodded. "Did you hear that dog outside a while ago? I never heard anything like that."

"That's Repeat," the store owner responded.

"Repeat?"

"Yeah, that's his name. You can hear that dog for miles. He belongs to an older couple that lives about a mile down that road." The store owner pointed across the highway to a blacktop road. Merle looked around at the road and nodded.

"Then, Repeat's not that kids dog?"

"No, Repeat and the kid are together every time the kid comes for a visit. He's the Krebs' grandson. He visits every summer. He'll be leaving Friday Mr. Krebs said. Kid lives in Dallas."

Merle Finch drove out of the store's parking area, crossed the highway, then drove a mile down the blacktop road. He pulled over the side of the road, got out, climbed up on the bed of the truck, shielded his eyes, and scanned the area. He saw the house about five hundred yards off the road. "That's it," he said. "That's where big bark lives."

He looked all around and studied the area....

Chapter 10

THE HEAVY EGG

Tuesday morning; three more days. Steven was counting down until his new life in the city would begin. Today, he would play some computer games and think about the things he would do back in the city with his new power. A power that was just his. No one could mess with him now. If anyone did, he would soon find out he was wasting his time. Now, Steve Wayne Krebs could not be touched by anyone.

Steven and Grandpa went to the barn to tend to the chores. Finished, they went to breakfast and then Steven went to the guest room and opened his laptop. He'd play some computer games today and pass the time until Mom and Dad returned from Paris and came for him. He was about to load a game when Grandma knocked on the guest room door. Steven opened it.

"Stevie, you're still here. I'm about to feed the chickens and gather the eggs would...

"I'll help you, Grandma," Steven said. Steven followed her to the kitchen. Grandma handed him a basket with a white cloth spread in the bottom. She picked up a small pail. Steven leaned over and looked inside it. It was a third full of small green pellets. They looked like grass that had been pressed down into pellets. Grandma went out the back door. Steven followed.

Grandma stepped out on the small back porch then began calling the chickens. "Here, chick, chick, chick, here chick." Steven saw the chickens come running toward the porch from all directions. Grandma reached into the pail and grasped a handful of the feed and threw it across the yard. The chickens changed direction and headed for the feed. They began pecking the ground rapidly. Grandma threw out several hands full then turned to Steven.

"Okay, go and get the eggs. There's a large nest inside the chicken house, in the corner. There's a bank of nests attached to the side of it, and another bank of nests there." Grandma pointed to the left of the chicken house at an enclosure with ten cubby-holes mounted a couple of feet above the ground between the chicken house and the storage shed. Steven went into the chicken house and looked across from the chicken's roost. There was a larger nest surrounded with hay. Inside it was five eggs. He gathered them and placed them in his basket. He checked the nest attached to the building and gathered a dozen more then went to the free standing enclosure.

Going down the nests gathering one to three eggs in each nest, he picked up an egg that was much heavier than the others. He turned it over and over in his hand, looking at it. He turned to Grandma.

"Grandma, this egg is real heavy." Grandma came over to the bank of nests and looked at the egg.

"Stevie, that's a chalk egg." Steven frowned and looked around at the flock of chickens pecking the ground. "One of the chickens laid a chalk egg!"

Grandma chuckled. "No, I bought it at the feed store and put it in the nest."

"Why?" Steven said.

"The chalk egg in the nest makes the chickens think it a good place to lay her eggs, since there's already one there."

Steven looked at the chickens again. "They don't know it's not a real egg?"

"Stevie, to a chicken, if it's the shape of an egg and the size of an egg; it's an egg."

"No wonder they jerk their heads when they walk; they're dumb." Grandma laughed. Steven smiled, gathered the remaining eggs and handed the basket to his grandma. She went back into the house. Steven glanced at the corner of the house. Repeat was sitting there waiting for Grandma to finish the chore. He never interfered with the cows or chickens. Steven thought about that for a moment.

Grandpa sure knows how to handle dogs. He knows a lot of stuff. Of course, he's had a long time to learn.

Steven returned to the guest room, opened his laptop and began looking through his game CD's. He heard the phone ring, then Grandmother answering it. Moments later, she knocked on Steven's door. He opened it.

"Stevie, that was the store manager over on the highway. He wants me to come by and pick up the money from several of my items that have sold. Let's drive over to the store. You can bring Repeat.

Grandma drove to the store, parked and went inside. Steven patted Repeat on the head. "Wait here, boy," he said.

Steven got out of the car and went into the store behind Grandma. While Grandma was talking with the store manager, Steven went and looked at the Show and Sell racks. The short sleeve shirt section was almost empty. There was only a couple of shirts left. "Wow," he said. "People must really like the home-sewn clothing."

While Steven was looking at the clothing sales area, a man entered the store and quietly looked around. He was unable to see Steven standing behind the partition of the Show and Sell display. The man saw Grandma and the store manager settling Grandma's account.

The store manager was counting out the money owed Grandma.

The man, glancing around the store again, reached inside his jacket and pulled out a gun, and then approached the store manager, holding the weapon at the ready. Grandma Krebs gasped and backed away a couple of steps.

"Just relax, Grandma," the man said. "All I need is the money out of that cash register." The man stood staring at the store manager. The store manager looked at the man's face then at the gun in his hand. "Sure, sure, it's yours."

The manager quickly stepped over to the cash register and tapped a key to open the money drawer.

Steven heard the man address his grandmother then say he wanted the money from the cash register. Steven peeked around the partition and saw the man holding a gun with it pointed at the store manager. He quietly slipped the device out of his pocket and pointed it at the intruder and pushed the button. The man collapsed instantly to a sitting position and then fell over on his side. The gun fell to the floor. When it hit, it fired, smashing a light in the ceiling of the store. Grandma's hand went to her mouth; she stared at the sleeping gunman, then glanced at Steven. She ran over and grabbed Steven by the hand and dragged him out of the store. Out front, she forcibly put Steven behind her; shielding him for the sleeping figure. Steven was surprised at how strong his grandmother was.

The store manager, observing the man on the floor, apparently unconscious, grabbed the phone and called the sheriff. Less than ten minutes later a sheriff's deputy drove up with his rotating red beacon flashing, pulled his weapon, and entered the store. The store manager pointed at the sleeping gunman. The deputy glanced around the store and approached the sleeping form, saw the gun lying beside him, pushed the gun farther away from the man with his foot, and then confirmed the would-be robber was indeed asleep. He holstered his weapon, cuffed the man, then picked up the weapon with two fingers on the barrel and went outside to his patrol car. When Grandma saw the deputy had cuffed the character she released Steven and hugged him. Steven stepped over to get a visual of the sleeping man. The coast was clear. He cupped the device in his hands, pointed it, and pushed the button again. The sleeping man, sat up, realized he was handcuffed, then looked all around the store. He saw the police car outside then looked up at the store manager.

"What happened?"

The store manager smiled. "Looks like all the excitement got to you; you apparently fainted." The deputy saw the intruder sitting up, pitched the radio mike into the seat then went into the store to arrest him. The store manager looked at Grandma Krebs.

"Where were we?" the store manager said. Grandma joined him at the cash register.

"I can't believe that," she said.

"That's the second time that's happened," the store manager said. "A couple of years ago, a guy came in here the same way. He took off with three hundred and six dollars. They caught him though, down by the river."

Steven watched his grandma and the store manager for a moment. They were safe and tending to business. He liked the feeling of saving his grandmother and the store man, although they could never know that he was responsible for 'saving the day.' Steven went back to the car, put Repeat back in the floor board, then joined him in the car. He petted Repeat on the head.

Steven felt good about his new power and what it could do.

Chapter 11

SECRET POWER

"Stevie, you come back and see us any time you want to," Grandma Krebs said, hugging him and rubbing her warm hand in his hair.

"I will, Grandma," Steven said. "I had fun exploring in the woods and stuff with Repeat." Steven hugged his grandfather and got in the car, eager to get back to the city. Steven's father got in the car and glanced at Steven in the back seat.

"Dad," Steven said, "what does it mean to watch your 'P's and 'Q's?"

Steven's dad smiled. "Grandma, huh."

"Yeah, Grandma told me to watch my 'P's and 'Q's when I went out exploring with Repeat."

His father smiled, looked out the windshield of the car at Steven's grandmother and mother talking, then back to Steven. "You can type pretty fast on a computer keyboard, can't you, Son."

Steven frowned. "Yeah, I can type eighty words a minute."

"Do you ever miss any letters?"

"Sometimes, but not very much."

"When you do miss letters, which ones are they, usually?"

Steven eye's widened. 'P's and 'Q's!" Steven looked out the windshield at his grandmother and mother then back to his dad. "I didn't know that people from the old days were that smart."

His father winked. "There's different kinds of smart."

Steven's mother got in the car and asked Steven that mother's question. "Did you have fun, Sweetheart?"

"Yes, Mom, it was great."

Dallas, Texas

Steven hurried to his room, put his two suitcases on the bed and looked around. His room was smaller; no, it was the same; he was bigger, now. He pulled the device out of his pocket and looked at it.

It was real, he still had it, and he was back in his own room.

Steven gripped it, put it back in his pocket, and started unpacking his suitcases. Things would be different now. When he went down the street to the park and the guys came around, those that always mocked him and pushed him around, he'd have a surprise for them. They wouldn't be pushing Steven Wayne Krebs around anymore. After all, you can't be mean when you are sound asleep. Steven laughed out loud.

He'd have to fix his 'laser' so nobody would notice it in his hand when he took it out of his pocket to 'zap' the bad guys. He took it out of his pocket again and looked at it. He'd have to think of some way to conceal it so no one would know that he had it. He knew that if he took it out of his pocket every time he used it, sooner or later, someone would see it, ask what it is, and then talk about it. It wouldn't be long until everybody would know that he had it. If that happened, the adults would take it away and Steven would be like he was before…

Helpless.

Maybe he could cut a hole in his pocket to stick it through. Steven caught his breath. Maybe it would work through his clothes! If it would, he wouldn't have to take it out of his pocket. Steven hurried outside into the back yard. When he stepped out of the door one of the neighborhood squirrels scampered across the yard to the back fence and stopped; frozen in a ready-to-go stance. A gentle breeze ruffled the hair on the creature's bushy tail. Steven, his hand in his pocket, rotated the device in the direction of the agile creature, and pushed the button.

The squirrel collapsed instantly. Steven took the device out of his pocket and gripped it again.

It would work through his clothes!

He went over to the squirrel, squat down and looked at it closely. He reached down and pulled the tiny lips apart and looked the creature's teeth. He was surprised at how sharp and vicious they looked for such a small and beautiful animal.

"Steven," he heard his mother call from the back door, "Dinner's ready." Startled, Steven jumped up and turned around.

"Okay, Mom." His mother disappeared from the back door. Steven turned back to the squirrel, positioned the device, and pushed the button. The squirrel jumped up and raced down the back fence and up the tree in the corner of the yard in seconds.

Steven patted his pocket. The device would work through his clothes. No one would ever know that he had it. No one would know that Steven Krebs had the power, just him, to use it any way he wanted.

Chapter 12

THE PARK

Steven woke up Saturday morning to the sounds of the city. He hopped out of bed, dressed, and went to the kitchen. His dad was already dressed to leave for the office. He was sitting at the table sipping a cup of coffee and reading the paper. He glanced up when Steven came into the room.

"Good morning, Son. You're up early. Two weeks in the country did you some good, huh."

"Good morning, Dad, can I have some coffee?" He was more mature now, perhaps it was time he started drinking coffee.

His dad looked at him. "You're too young, Son, and coffee is strong. Here, you can taste it but I don't want you to start drinking coffee just yet. Stay with orange juice and milk a while longer." Steven took the cup, held it close to his mouth and blew on the liquid as he had seen his grandmother do, then took a sip. "Uuuuk!" he said, pushing the cup away. "That's bitter."

His father chuckled. "It is at first but, when you get used to it, it's delicious."

"How can you get used to something that taste so bad?"

His father smiled. "You'll see when you get older. When you start living life as an adult, coffee will start your day off right."

Steven wondered what happened to the taste buds when you grow up. Another mystery, like the tree frogs getting up in trees and hollering all night. Steven took a sip of orange juice; much better.

Steven's dad left for the office. He said he had a couple of meetings to conclude a piece of business from the Paris Conference. Mom was on the phone with one of her friends. As Steven finished his meal, he noticed the sound of an airliner in the distance. All the sounds of the city were still there. He got up from the table and headed for the front door. "Mom, I'm going to the park for a while, okay."

"Okay, Sweetheart, be careful and watch the traffic."

"Mom, I'm almost thirteen," Steven said.

"I know, Steven, and you're smart. Just be careful, okay."

"I will, Mom," Steven said as he went out the front door.

Steven started his usual route to the park; the same one he took to walk the five blocks to school. He came to the place where he always crossed the street to avoid the penned-in Doberman on the left of the walkway. The animal was mean and vicious. The fence was high enough that he couldn't get out and actually attack, but Steven didn't like the mean vicious growling and barking as he walked by. He couldn't understand why somebody would keep a dog like that; but the old man did. Everybody said he was a hermit and didn't like people coming around. He kept the dog to keep the people away.

Steven stopped in the middle of the street. He didn't have to avoid him anymore. He could just shut the mean animal up. He'd put him to sleep, then wake him up later if he was still asleep the next time he saw him. Steven retraced his steps and walked straight down the sidewalk that went right by the yard where the Doberman was kept. The dog was used to standing near the fence and watching Steven walk by on the other side of the street all during school. When the animal smelled Steven coming, he assumed his usual posture to wait for the *routine*.

When Steven appeared at the corner of the yard, just on the other side of the fence this time the Doberman went crazy. He began barking, growling viciously, and jumping against the fence. Steven jumped back in an automatic reflex then regained control. He rotated the device in his pocket and pushed the button. The large animal was asleep in the middle of a jump. He landed straight up on his belly, his front legs apart, with his chin on the grass. His eyes were closed. His breathing was deep and regular. Steven smiled. "Night, night."

Steven resumed his walk to the park. He noticed the sounds of the cars driving by from time to time and the distant sounds of the city. He heard a siren wale far in the distance. A world without fear from now on. He sighed as he crossed the street into the park. He looked around and saw no one. This was the first time he'd come to the park this early. He had it all to himself. He walked out into the area with the climbing maze, the wooden pirate ship, the swings, slides, and tether ball poles. He pushed one of the swings and watched it swing until it stopped. He knocked the tether ball around the stationary pole for some time. Then, he heard them.

Hey, Twerp!" Steven spun around. It was the three bullies from school. They smarted off to everybody and pushed everybody around all the time. They were bigger than everybody else in the class and always had a sneer on their faces and rubbed it in that they were big and nobody in the class could stop them.

Bruce Johnson was the leader, 'Buzz' to his sidekicks. He was six inches taller that Steven; stocky. He was fourteen and he smoked. Charlie Rockford; Steven's height, fat, 'Rocky' to his peers. And the one with the smartest mouth; tall as Buzz, but real skinny; Virgil Simmons, 'Verge;' he smoked, too.

The three stepped off the side walk into the park and started toward Steven. Buzz spoke first: "Your mother let you out of the yard this early?"

Verge chimed in: "Hey, Buzz, maybe his *mommy* couldn't stand his ugly face no longer." The three bullies laughed and jeered at Steven as they approached him.

Steven nervously tried to get his hand in his pocket. He missed the opening several times, then, finding it, he gripped the device, rotated it in the direction of the three advancing teens and pushed the button. The three bullies collapsed instantly, falling headlong on the grass. Steven, breathing heavily, backed away several steps and looked around. He saw no one. He slowly walked up to the three sleeping forms and looked at them. Their faces showed no pain, just peaceful sleep. Their breathing was deep and regular.

Steven felt strange. It wasn't like he thought it would be. He backed away from the three teens, looked around again; still no one.

He took the device out of his pocket and looked at it for a moment then back at the three figures sprawled out on the grass. They looked completely and totally helpless. There was something eerie about it. Steven took a deep breath, walked over to the sidewalk, then turned around and pointed the device at the three sleepers. He hesitated for a moment, then, pushed the button.

The three awakened bullies sat up immediately, looked at each other, confused, they began brushing the freshly mowed bits of grass from their faces.

"What happened?" Rocky said, looking at his friends faces, wiping the grass clippings from his own.

"I don't know," Buzz said as he got to his feet and wiped the grass from his clothes. "Where's the twerp."

Steven was already running down the sidewalk toward home.

"There he goes!" Rocky said. Verge cupped his hand around his mouth.

"You better go home, Twerp, and stay there!"

Steven sat in his room. He'd stopped the bullies that had always picked on him, made fun of him, and mocked him. He'd stopped them cold. But he didn't feel good about it. Why? They had it coming. They were wrong to pick on him because they were bigger and could do it. Then why was he feeling bad about it? They should be put to sleep every time they started doing people like that. Pretty soon they would stop doing it to get to stay awake.

But still, it didn't seem right.

Steven Wayne Krebs sat in the silence of his thoughts for some time. Then, as if a weight was lifted off his shoulders, he came to a decision.

He wouldn't zap anybody else.

Unless he just *had* too.

Steven turned on his computer, went on the Net, then began touching on the web sites he frequented as a matter of routine. As the day wore on he'd updated himself on the activity that had transpired in the two weeks that he had been out of town and out of touch. Suddenly a promise came to the front of his mind. "The Doberman!" he said out loud. He'd forgotten about the Doberman he'd put to sleep hours ago. He turned off his computer and headed out the front door. The dog had been sleeping for hours now, unless he woke up after sleeping for a while. He would soon know. Up until now he had immediately awakened everything he had put to sleep. He'd never checked to see how long things would stay asleep once they had been zapped with the device.

He approached the yard where the large dog was kept and quietly peaked through the fence. The animal was still exactly where he fell when he'd put him to sleep. Steven moved on down the fence to look closely at the dog. The dog was breathing deep and regular and not moving at all. He noticed movement in the Doberman's nostrils. Something was coming out of one of his nose holes.

"Ants!" Steven gasped. Ants were going in and out of the dog's nose as he lay sleeping peacefully. Steven took out the device and looked at it momentarily, then aimed it at the Doberman and pushed the button. The animal jumped up, barked and growled at Steven, then started snorting and whining, rubbing its nose on the grass and rubbing his snout with his paws. The dog bounded around the yard, yelping and snorting for several minutes. Steven backed away from the yard, across the street and waited, watching the Doberman. A few minutes later the dog began to settle down. The animal headed for his water bowl and drank for a full minute, then looked around for Steven. Not seeing him, he laid down and rubbed his nose from time to time.

Steven had a disturbing feeling invade his mind. The device is serious, very serious. If you put something to sleep and don't wake it up, it will sleep until it dies. In regular sleep, that dog would have woke up when those ants crawled up in his nose. The sleep from the device is a different kind of sleep. Permanent sleep. He would have to be really responsible from now on and wake up everything he puts to sleep. Everything.

Chapter 13

KIDNAPPED

Merle Finch, breathing heavily from his last quarter of a mile carrying the sleeping dog, entered the training pen behind the mobile home of his cousin, Buford Thompson. He laid Repeat down on the ground, exited the door, closed and secured it, then staggered over and sat down on a wooden bench by the small back porch behind Buford's place. Buford stepped out the back door, glanced at the sleeping dog locked in the pen, then back to Merle.

"Cousin, where did you get that dog?" Buford asked, glancing again at Repeat lying on the ground. Repeat had begun to stir as the tranquilizing agent wore off.

Merle, after catching his breath, looked up at cousin Buford. "About two or three miles through those woods," he said pointing toward the north. "He was hanging around an older couple's house. The store manager told me he came up to the Krebs farm as a stray and they just adopted him, a couple of years ago."

"Why do you want him?" Buford asked. Repeat, now on his feet, licked his right hip where the tranquilizer dart had hit him, then his senses located the two men sitting behind the mobile home, talking.

Repeat barked that loud penetrating bark—full force.

Buford fell off the porch and hit the end of the bench Merle was sitting on turning it over and dumping both men on the ground. "What was that!" Buford exclaimed.

"That, Cousin, is the sound of lots of money."

The balmy days of mid-summer were counting down to Steven's thirteenth birthday. He'd spent the first two weeks of summer vacation from school at Grandpa and Grandma's house. "*Well worth the time,*" Steven thought, patting his pocket. And, now, in two days, he'd finally be thirteen; a teenager. He thought about Repeat and their adventures together. Maybe he should get a dog here in the city. "*No,*" he thought. It wouldn't be the same. Repeat was smart, Repeat listened to everything you said. Repeat knows how to explore and stuff. Steven took a breath.

Maybe he could bring Repeat here to the city. They could explore lots of stuff here, and, he had the device if they needed it. If things got bad or something. He'd have to talk to

Grandpa, Grandma, Dad, and Mom. He'd think about that. He'd have to know what to say. Repeat, right here at home; here in the city.

Steven tried to look cool sitting around the dining room table with a group of his 'Pentium Class' friends. The name, Pentium Class, was decided upon by the group to give themselves a club name. They were all nerds of their own confession. They were smart and had report cards to back that up; they were very good on computers and everyone knew that. Most of them hand been asked by other classmates and even their parents how to handle various computer issues.

Steven glanced from friend to friend. None of them knew about the device. There had not been a point of interaction with any of them since he had found the device. Besides, he wasn't so sure that his friends could keep it a secret. It was so enticing that one of them might slip. And if they did, it would be over. He couldn't take that chance; not yet. He had just found out that its sleep-inducing influence was permanent. That's serious; very serious. He wasn't sure that they would understand how serious it is. He'd best keep the device secret.

The birthday song rang through the kitchen. Steven was careful not to grimace. Steven's friends were smart but they could not sing. However, they were his friends and he knew they were sincere and real. He smiled awkwardly when they finished and then watched him blow out the thirteen candles in one breath. Everyone cheered and clapped.

Then came the presents. He unwrapped an assortment of a shirt, a CD holder, a belt, a pen and pencil set, and even a pair of socks. Pentium class friends were smart; not cool.

"Steven, phone for you," Steven heard his mother call from the kitchen, "it's your grandmother." Steven excused himself from the party and went to his room to talk to his grandmother. He didn't want his friends to hear him. Grandmas always get mushy. Besides, somebody had to be cool on his birthday. He closed the door and picked up the phone.

"Hi, Grandma."

"Steven," came from the phone, "happy birthday. You're thirteen now. Your grandpa and I wanted to wish you a happy birthday and tell you again that we enjoyed your visit."

"It was great, Grandma. How's Repeat doing?" There was a pause on the phone. "Grandma?"

Grandma's voice continued: "I'm sorry, Stevie, but Repeat's gone."

Steven paused and took a couple of breaths. "Repeat died!"

"Oh, no," Grandma said, "he just disappeared. Your grandfather walked around the farm as much as he could, calling him, but he never came. He must have run away."

"Grandma," Steven said seriously, "Repeat would not run away."

"Stevie, Sweetheart," his grandmother said gently, "he's gone. We miss him too, but he's gone."

"Repeat would not run away. Somebody had to take him; kidnap him. I know Repeat, Grandma, he would not run away."

"Steven, you have to accept...

"Grandma," Steven interrupted, "I'm coming down there and look for him. I know he would not run away. Something is wrong. Somebody took him and I'm going to find him."

By late afternoon Steven was sitting in his father's home office, pleading his case: "Dad, I could ride the bus to Grandma's house. I've got eighty dollars saved up. I'm thirteen now."

Steven's dad held his eyes for a moment. "You believe that someone took Repeat. You don't think that the dog just ran away. You know, Son, that Repeat was a stray when he came to your grandparent's house in the first place."

"I know," Steven said. "But, Dad, Repeat and me became friends, good friends, while we were exploring the woods. I know him. He would not run away; I'm telling you, Dad; he would not run away. Something is wrong and I want to see if I can find him."

Steven's dad studied his face for a long moment. "Let me talk to your mother. Meet me here tomorrow afternoon when I get home from the office."

"Okay," Steven said anxiously, "thanks, Dad.' Steven went to the door of the office and opened it then turned to his father: "Repeat would not run away." His dad studied Steven's face for a moment, then nodded.

Steven sat on the side of his bed, deep in thought. His mind began working on the problem of how he could find out what happened to Repeat. He could not imagine Repeat leaving Grandpa's and Grandma's house. Repeat loved being there. He had his favorite spots and a whole farm to romp and play on, and, he was Steven's friend. He had become Steven's best friend, beginning last summer when they had met for the first time, and then this summer when they explored everywhere together. He knew Repeat better than anybody. Repeat would not run away. He had to find him.

Chapter 14

THE MISSION

Donald and Rhonda Krebs sat in their bedroom in conference on something new; Steven's request to travel to his grandparent's farm alone. Donald outlined what he and Steven had discussed earlier in his home office.

Rhonda took a breath. "There's something special about his wanting to go and take action on Repeat's behalf. Another thing, I like him out of his room and doing things instead of sitting in there on his computer all summer."

Donald nodded. "I thought about that. This would be a good experience for him to learn to take care of himself and pay attention to the things around him."

"I would want to talk to him every day," Rhonda said.

"I'd feel better if I did, too.

"Tell him he has to call every day,"

"I will. By the way, in case you haven't noticed; your son is growing up." Rhonda smiled.

Steven climbed up the steps into the bus at the Dallas terminal, went to the back and sat down. He was on his own and wanted everyone to be in front of him so he could see them all. He had to pay attention to everything around him, he was alone and had to watch out for himself. His Dad had cautioned him to watch the buses progress as it made the several stops before reaching his destination, Clarksville, Texas, where Grandma and Grandma would pick him up at the bus station. Steven had checked out the bus schedule, and the stops it would make, on the Internet before he left home. He must check everything because he didn't want to do something really dumb like getting off the bus in the wrong town.

His dad had said something that had stuck in his mind. *"All forests look alike when you are standing among the trees."* Steven would count the stops and identify the towns.

The bus pulled out of the station and began making its way through the traffic to the freeway and its first leg of the journey. The journey to Grandma's house and the mission to find Repeat and bring him back home.

Steven now had two devices, one in each pocket. His secret device in one and a quarter sized brass encased compass in the other, presented to him by his dad just before boarding the bus. "You never know," his dad had said.

Steven began thinking about what to do first when he got to Grandma's house. Repeat was missing and nobody knew why of even exactly when he had disappeared. If someone took him, which Steven believed happened, there had to be a reason why. What would anyone see in Repeat that would make them want to steal him. He was just an ordinary dog. You could go to the pound and get all the dogs you want. You don't have to steal one. There would have to be something special, very special, about a dog to warrant all the trouble, and to take the risk. Steven snapped to attention. "Repeat's bark!" he said loudly.

Several fellow passengers turned and looked at Steven momentarily, then went back to their own affairs.

"Repeat's bark," Steven repeated quietly. "That's got to be it. It's the only thing that special about him. You can hear Repeat's bark for miles. But why would someone steal him to get the loud bark. Most people would be irritated by it. Grandpa got on to Repeat several times about barking so loud and scaring the cows. Repeat did pretty good, but sometimes he would forget. Grandpa would give him that *look*; Repeat would make the correction. After a while the cows had gotten used to it."

Steven hesitated. "Okay," he said, "We proceed as if someone sneaked up to the farm and took Repeat. Where and how would he...."

The bus slowed and exited the interstate, interrupting his thoughts. Steven came to attention and looked all around the area. The bus drove away from the interstate about a quarter of a mile and entered a small town and pulled up in front of a service station. On one side of the building was a glassed in room with vending machines and a desk with a large bulletin board behind it. *"A small town bus station,"* Steven thought. *"Stop number one."*

The bus remained parked for about ten minutes. Two people got on the bus; a lady that sat down in the second seat from the front and an older man that made his way to the back and sat down next to Steven. He looked as old as his grandpa. He had a small carry-on suitcase. He slid it under the seat, glanced at Steven and nodded. Steven smiled and then looked up when the bus began moving. Moments later the bus was back on the interstate and resuming highway speed. The mission was back on. Stop number one done, two more to go, then the final destination and the quest.

Steven went back to his thoughts of how to proceed. He wondered how someone would be able to approach his grandparent's farm and take Repeat. If someone tried to grab Repeat, he would notify everyone in a mile radius. He was that loud. That wouldn't work. Steven said to himself, *"Repeat wouldn't go with somebody he didn't know. He would..."*

"Young man," the older man said to Steven. Steven's mind came back to the moment. He looked at the man and smiled. "Yes, Sir?"

The old man looked a Steven with kind gentle eyes. "You seem to be wrestling with something, like something's bothering you; can I help? I'm a good listener; I've been doing it a long, long, time. My name's John; John Cassidy; everybody calls me JC." He extended his hand; Steven took it and shook hands.

"I'm going to my grandparent's house." Steven volunteered.

"Are your grandma and grandpa okay?" Steven nodded. JC smiled and nodded. "Well, it's good that you are going to see them. I'm sure they will be happy to see you."

"I was there a week ago," Steven said. JC raised an eyebrow. Steven continued. "I'm going back because my friend is missing and I want to see if I can find him."

"Your friend?"

"Repeat. He's a dog; Grandpa's dog. He went missing and I'm going back to see if I can find him."

"Oh. Well, that's a noble quest. I had a dog when I was your age. Best friend I ever had. We were always together. His name was Streak. He was the fastest dog in the county. He could run like the wind. He finally grew old and died."

"Repeat's young," Steven said quickly.

"Repeat?"

Steven smiled and nodded. "That's his name." Steven went on to tell JC the story of Repeat's special name. JC chuckled.

"You think somebody took him?" JC inquired.

"Yeah," Steven said. "I think someone took him because of his bark. He's just an average dog, but he's got a bark louder that a Doberman or a Saint Bernard."

"That loud, huh?"

Steven nodded. "You wouldn't believe how much sound comes from a dog that small."

"Well," JC offered, "if somebody wanted a hunting dog that you could hear from a distance, sounds like Repeat would be ideal. Or if a carnival barker wanted a dog he could bill as the loudest dog in the world...who knows." Steven's mind went back to the carnival momentarily. No, the carnival was gone when he and his mom and dad drove through town on their way home. He saw the empty grounds where it had been set up.

What he would do is search the farm and look for evidence that might give him a clue. Dad had put no limit on his stay as long as he called every day and talked to his mother. A thought popped into Steven's mind.

"Mr. Cassidy...ah, JC, I want to ask you something." JC nodded. Steven continued: "How would somebody keep Repeat quiet when they took him. With his bark, you could hear him for miles. Grandpa would know something was wrong and call the sheriff. Repeat would not volunteer to go with someone he didn't know. When they tried to force him, he'd sound off."

"Well," JC said, "there's only one way. You can't sneak up on a dog. Their noses work too good and their ears just as good. You would have to shot him with a tranquilizer gun, a dart, and put him to sleep. Then you could just pick him up and take him away." Steven sat straight up.

"A tranquilizer dart!" he exclaimed. "That has to be the way that they did it."

"Steven," JC said, "look for a crimped cartridge that will be lying on the ground where he did it; if that's what happened."

"What's a crimped cartridge?" Steven said.

"Have you ever seen a bullet?" Steven nodded. "My dad has a souvenir Army rifle and some bullets."

"A crimped cartridge will be a bullet with the slug removed from the end of it and the end crimped closed with the powder still in the shell. The crimped cartridge is the force that propels the tranquilizer dart. The tranquilizer gun will eject the cartridge where it's fired. If you're lucky, you'll find it lying on the ground."

The bus slowed and exited the Interstate, drove down the service road, and stopped at a small bus station. John Cassidy got up, picked up his small suitcase and turned to Steven.

"This is my stop. It was good talking with you. I hope you find your dog. Best friends are hard to find." Steven smiled and took JC's hand when it was extended.

"I'll find him," Steven vowed. "When you do," JC said, "give him a big hug for me. I still miss my dog; best friend I ever had."

The bus driver finished updating his records, then opened the bus door and announced a fifteen-minute stop and exited the bus. Steven, hearing the announcement, picked up his small bag and got off the bus. He went inside to the vending machine and got a Coke. He opened it and took a swallow, then walked over to the big picture window and made a mental note of the number on 'his' bus. He wanted to be sure to get back on the right bus, just in case they moved it to put fuel in it or something. He had to think of everything himself. There was no one watching over him and there always had been up until now. Before this trip to Grandma's by himself, there had always been someone tending to everything; his parents, or the people at school. He liked the feeling of being on his own and keeping up with everything.

The bus finally left the Interstate and began the leg of the journey on the old two lane road he'd traveled with his parents earlier. The bus seemed wider than the highway lane. The miles slowly went by the large vehicle as the scenes of the trails he would search played in his mind. He had a lot of ground to cover and he would be looking for something very small. A difficult task but he had to try. He tried to imagine what Repeat was doing right now. He could form no image. Repeat had always been free. He would be again, Steven vowed.

A few miles further the bus slowed and entered a small town and stopped at a convenience store and bus station combination. The driver opened the door and two people, who had already made their way down the aisle, got off. The driver closed the door and drove on. Stop number three; done; next stop; Clarksville.

As the bus continued its next leg to Clarksville, Steven began to anticipate the adventure of the search. It sure was going to be different walking all those trails without Repeat sniffing around him and barking and whining at different things. He already missed Repeat and he hadn't even arrived yet. But, thanks to an older, new-found friend, he knew what to look for and if he was lucky enough to actually find it; it would be hard evidence that Repeat didn't just leave and go somewhere else. Repeat wouldn't.

"I'll find him," he said under his breath.

Chapter 15

THE CLEARING

Steven awakened bright and early Tuesday morning in Grandma's guest room. He sat up, looked around, then jumped out of bed, dressed, and went into the kitchen. Grandma was about to start breakfast and Grandpa was on his way out the door to feed the animals and do the milking. Steven followed. When Grandpa began the chore of milking the cows Steven looked all around the corral and then looked at his grandfather.

"Grandpa, how long has Repeat been gone?" Grandpa glanced at Steven.

"Best I can tell, Steven, about a week." Steven noticed that his grandfather called him Steven instead of Stevie. Maybe it was because he was older now. Or, maybe it was because something 'grown-up' had happened in Steven's life. Something that violated the child's world, where a happy ending is arranged for everything. Perhaps this was his first real taste of reality that might not turn out so happy. He liked being addressed as Steven; however, a seriousness settled in his thoughts. After a moment Grandpa continued:

"Do you really think that somebody took Repeat?"

"Yeah, Grandpa, I do. I just can't see Repeat taking off to some other place. He really liked it here. I scolded him sometimes but I petted him a lot, too."

"Steven, don't worry about Repeat getting upset when you get onto him or scold him. Dogs are pack animals. They want to know whose boss. Between you and Repeat, that would be you. To Repeat, you are Alpha. When you scold him or correct him, he knows you are the boss and will follow you and protect you. He will feel secure and loved."

"Then I know he would not run away," Steven said positively, "and I'm going to find him."

"I hope you do. I think it would be a miracle. We sure miss him. We had gotten used to his being here. It seems like there's an empty space here on the farm. You know, I have a problem believing Repeat would just leave. But, we figured that's what must have happened. Whoever heard of an ordinary dog getting kidnapped?"

"Repeat's no ordinary dog, Grandpa. His bark…"

"Is loud," Grandpa interjected. "Very loud. You're right; when Repeat opens his mouth he's definitely not an ordinary dog. Do you think his bark got him taken?"

"Yeah, I do," Steven said. "I know he wouldn't leave and that's the only thing special about him. I'm going to retrace all the trails we walked together; all the places we explored and see if I can find any clues."

"Well, I wish I was young enough to walk them with you. I wish you luck. If Repeat's truly in trouble, he's lucky to have you for a friend."

"I'll find him, Grandpa. I'll find him and bring him home."

Steven went out the front door to begin the quest. He glanced at the spot where Repeat always laid down, then headed around the house and down to the creek. The first place he wanted to check was where they found the device. He believed that Repeat would remember that particular place and maybe go back there again because he and Repeat had made the discovery together. Alpha and Repeat. Steven hurried his steps. Grandpa knew lots of stuff about everything. Steven now had a deeper understanding of his and Repeat's relationship. He had to find him.

Steven crawled through the fence and continued to follow the creek, looking for the spot where he and Repeat had turned into the deep woods. About a hundred yards farther down the creek he noticed buzzards circling high in the air across the creek. There was three of them, huge birds with long wings, spiraling down in a 'holding' pattern.

"That means that there's something dead on the ground over there," Steven muttered. Suddenly a lump formed in Steven's throat. He stopped and looked again at the larger birds. "Oh, no," he said aloud, "not Repeat!" He cupped his hands around his mouth and shouted: "Repeeeat!" and listened; then again and listened; nothing; no response. He looked down at the creek. It was too wide to cross here. He could wade through it…wait. He ran back to the fence and crawled through. The creek was four feet wide here. He backed up a few steps, ran and jumped it, crawled back through the fence, took out the device and ran back toward where the buzzards were expressing their interest. As he approached, the buzzards broke off and flew a safe distance away to wait patiently for their 'provided' meal. Steven searched the ground from bush to bush and in the tall grass. Finally, he spotted it. It was a large crow; probably got in a fight with a hawk or something and lost.

Steven let out a sigh of relief and headed back for the fence and access to the other side of the creek and the deep woods, then the clearing where he and Repeat found the device.

Merle Finch sat on the wooden back porch of Cousin Buford's mobile home, sipping a cup of coffee and watching Big Bark finally sniff at the steak he'd tossed in his training pen earlier. The stubborn dog had eaten a little when he first took him, but now had refused to eat anything for two days. He had spirit. Good. He'd make a good fighter on the dog fighting circuit. Big Bark, Repeat, the old man had named him, finally ate the steak and drank some more water.

Merle would have to take Big Bark up-state to Chicago to put him on the circuit after he got him trained and ready to perform. The cops were looking for him here in Texas. They had nearly nabbed him during the last fighting session he'd sponsored. Merle had even seen his own picture on a TV special about animal cruelty. He was listed as an animal abuser wanted by the police. It was a 'if you see this man, call', and gave a number. He had to get Big Bark trained and out of here soon. He walked out to his truck, opened the storage box behind the cab and took out his padded trainer's suit and his light hollow cane stick and laid them on the porch. The special hollow cane stick was light enough that it wouldn't do any damage when he hit the dog; however, you keep hitting him with it and he'll get mad…mad enough to fight. He looked at Repeat standing *in the pen looking back at Merle. "A couple of days, Big Bark, a couple of days."*

Steven walked out into the clearing and looked around. The deer feeder was still there and still 'stocked' with a mixture of feed. Steven went straight to the bush where the device was found. He squatted down without thinking and pushed the branches apart again as he had done before. Of course, the device wasn't there; he had it in his pocket. He stood up, cupped his hands again and called to Repeat a couple of times. No response. He then walked toward the deer feeder as he had done the day they found the device and then over to the log and sat down for a few minutes.

"Okay," he said. "If somebody shot Repeat with a tranquilizer gun, he'd be pretty far away, maybe out at the edge of the clearing." Steven got up and began a detailed search around the edge of the clearing; looking for a crimped cartridge lying on the ground. The pace was slow, he wanted to be sure he didn't miss it and never know it. As the day wore on, he finally completed the full circumference of the clearing with no results. He sat down on the log again.

"This guy could have shot Repeat anywhere," Steven murmured. Tomorrow he would systematically check all the areas they, he and Repeat, had explored. He believed Repeat would re-visit all those trails after Steven was gone. Steven's scent would still be there and dogs are big on smell.

Tomorrow was another day and another quest. *"Repeat, I'm coming,"* he thought.

Steven, back at his grandma's house with the evening sun about to touch the treetops, called home and talked to his mom at length, filling her in on the day's activities and the results. She expressed her disappointment and encouragement. Steven surprised her with a pep talk and assurance of eventual success. After all, this is only the first day.

Chapter 16

TRAILS

Steven sat on the side of the bed looking out the window waiting for dawn. He had awakened early and dressed. The full day of exercise yesterday had made him sleep soundly and awaken early. He felt a touch of soreness in his leg muscles but, somehow, it felt good. The tree frogs' chorus began to fade out and the birds began their debut for the day. The trees took shape in the gradually increasing light. The stars winked off as if to rest up for the coming night. Steven took a deep breath. There was something special about the dawn; a brand new beginning. He thought of his quest with a new vigor.

Steven joined his grandfather for his morning routine of life on the farm. He was quiet for a while during the milking, then he spoke: "Grandpa, dogs have really keen senses, don't they?"

Grandpa glanced at Steven then back to his chore. "Yes, they do. In fact, no one knows just how capable they are. I read in a magazine article that some dogs in the city have heard their master's car entering the neighborhood when they are coming home from a quarter mile away. And, that's with dozens of other cars running at the same time. It's amazing."

"And smell, too, huh. Dogs could follow rabbits by smell even after their tracks are gone."

"Oh, yes," Grandpa said. "Many times we've heard Repeat sounding off out in the woods. Probably because he's picked up a trail of a rabbit or a squirrel."

Steven stepped off the porch and headed for the old syrup mill. He wondered if Repeat went back to follow that jack rabbit's trail and try to find him. He already knows he can't catch him. However, he would chase him again. He would remember being within a foot of the rabbit at one time; not knowing that Steven and the device had arranged it.

Steven made his way down the hill and along the overgrown road until he reached the shed and fallen mill. All was quiet. He began to scan the area for tracks. The spot where he laid the rabbit still showed traces of tracks. He followed the rabbit's tracks, along with Repeats for about a hundred yards. Then Repeat's tracks stopped and the rabbit's continued. Steve followed them on to see if Repeat had picked up the trail further on. The tracks led to a fence around the farm. The rabbit's tracks stopped a good ten feet from the fence. Steven crawled through then searched the area. He picked up the rabbit's tracks again about fifteen feet from the fence, in line with the tracks he'd been following on the other side of the fence. The jack rabbit had jumped the fence at full speed, covering some twenty-five feet. Still no tracks left by Repeat. Just the same, Steven cupped his hands again and sounded off Repeat's name, twice. Nothing.

Steven returned to the syrup mill and began a detailed search around it for a crimped cartridge. He though it possible that Repeat smelled the spot where he had lain the rabbit and while smelling it, was shot by the kidnapper. He spiraled around the mill in an ever widening circle, studying the ground. After three trips around the mill and starting number four he suddenly heard a rustling in the weeds. He jumped back then pulled out the device and held it at the ready. He eased forward, reached and pushed the grass to one side. A black colored snake was coiled up, holding its head up flicking its tongue. Steven aimed the device and pushed the button. The snake's head fell down onto its coiled body. Steven looked closely. It was black, sort of gunmetal colored with a lighter underbelly. It was a Water Moccasin; poisonous, according to Grandpa. Steven pocketed the device and continued his search, also watching for snakes just to be safe.

Satisfied that there was no crimped cartridge around the mill, Steven concluded the search and started for home. He'd gone about a hundred yards when it occurred to him that he had some unfinished business back at the mill. He pulled out the device and headed back to wake up the snake. When he spotted it, he aimed the device:

"You're lucky to get this consideration, being a snake and all." Steven pushed the button and watched the snake raise its head and crawl away.

"It's a matter of principal," he said.

At lunch, Steven was filling Grandma in on the day's activities so far and reassuring her that the quest was still on. He would keep going until he found Repeat.

"I sure hope it's possible," Grandma said. "You deserve to find him if it can be done."

"Grandma," Steven said, "if something has happened to Repeat, I'd like to know. I don't like not knowing." Then Steven locked eyes with his grandmother. "If something has happened and Repeat is gone, dead, he deserves for someone to know."

Grandma blinked several times then nodded: "That's right, Steven, he does."

Steven noticed that Stevie, the child, was gone from Grandma's speech, too.

Steven crossed the pasture and crawled through the back fence and looked toward the deep woods. He doubted Repeat would go to the tree with the skunk's den, but he'd sniff around the rest of the trails they had made here. And, this is some distance from the house. If someone shot Repeat with a tranquilizer gun, more than likely, he'd want to be as far from the house as possible. He would not want the old couple to call the sheriff and report a gun shot on their property.

At the fence, Steven began his detailed search on both sides of the trail for evidence. Perhaps, tracks of a man, or the crimped cartridge that he was sure was here somewhere. Somewhere where Repeat had been. He systematically checked each side of the trail almost to the blackened tree where Repeat had learned something important about skunks. Steven smiled when he thought about Repeat's dilemma when the skunk sprayed him right on the nose. That was a day to remember.

Steven started back to the house. He had covered all the trails that he and Repeat had explored; all except up and down the creek right there close to the house. He believed that the culprit would do his deed much farther away. However, he would check it just the same. But, he had a growing feeling that the sight of the kidnapping was the clearing in the deep woods. It's so remote that it was an ideal place to tranquilize Repeat and then simply carry him off through the woods. No one would ever know. He would check the clearing again, much more thoroughly this time.

Steven walked up and down the creek from property line to property line, fence to fence, just to be sure he hadn't missed anything. He found nothing, which is, what he expected to find. For some reason he was sure he'd find answers at the clearing.

Late that evening, Steven called his mother. They talked for some time, Steven outlining his day and the trails he walked. He'd begin to explain himself fairly well. After a time, his dad came on the line.

"Dad," Steven said, "I need to know something."

"Okay."

"Did you ever go back to the clearing in the woods behind Grandma's house?"

"The deer blind?"

"Deer blind?" Steven said, "what's a deer blind."

"There's a deer feeder out in the clearing and…"

"I saw that," Steven interrupted. "It's a barrel on legs with animal feed in a pan."

"Well," his father continued, "the reason that feeder is there is to bring deer out in the open during hunting season. About twenty feet into the woods at the edge of the clearing, up in the top of a tree, is a deer blind. It's a small hut with a shooting window for hunters to wait for a good shot at a deer. It's called a deer blind because deer won't see it. Deer don't look up. They figure that all their enemies are on the ground. If I remember right, it's on the north side of the clearing. You've got your compass. But, Steven, you'll have to look carefully for it. It's built-in among branches to make it hard to see."

Steven hung up the phone. A new piece of information from an old explorer. The deer blind. That would be a perfect place for someone to hid and shoot Repeat with a tranquilizer rifle. Tomorrow he'd check it out.

Donald Krebs hung up the phone and leaned back in his chair in thought. There was something about Steven's changing from a 'hermit in his room' on his computer most of the time, to an active young man. It's amazing that two weeks in the country at his grandparents would have such a profound effect on him. Donald was glad to see it happen but wondered how it could be so dramatic. Perhaps Steven had become really attached to Repeat for some special reason. Just maybe Repeat had saved Steven's life or, perhaps, the other way around. Something that only they shared. He would talk to Steven often. There's something important happening here.

Chapter 17

THE TRAIL

Steven, sitting on the ground watching his grandfather tend to the cows, looked out across the farm toward the woods beyond. He turned to him. "Grandpa, did you ever go deer hunting?"

"Years ago," Grandpa said, glancing at Steven. "In fact, I took your father deer hunting when he was twelve."

"Did you and Dad go to the deer blind at the clearing?"

"How did you know about that?" Grandpa finished the milking and set the stool back in its place.

"I talked to Dad last night. I asked him if he'd been to the clearing I found in the woods. He told me about the deer blind. I'm going to check it out today just in case somebody hid in it and waited for Repeat."

'I see," Grandpa said. "It's worth a shot."

"When you and Dad went hunting; did Dad shoot a deer?" Grandpa studied Steven's face for a moment.

"Yes, he did. We got up in the deer blind about sundown. We had water and some jerky with us. We talked quietly about everything, all night. Just about dawn when first light crept into the woods a ten-point buck deer, rack a good two feet wide, walked up to the deer feeder and started eating. Your Dad leveled his rifle on the window seal, took aim, and squeezed the trigger. Got him just behind the fore-leg. Good shot."

Steven was spellbound listening his grandfather relate an age old scene that happened at a place Steven had been. A scene that played out many years ago.

"That experience changed your father. You know, he grew up in the days of Pac Man and Pen Ball machines. He played those games for hours every time he had the opportunity. Every time I went to town for feed and salt lick blocks for the cows he would play in the video parlors as long as he could. But, after getting the deer, seeing it dressed out and used for food, he changed. He began favoring the outdoors. Started exploring almost every day."

"I know," Steven said. "I have followed a bunch of his trails. He explored all over this farm."

Steven stepped off the porch, headed for the clearing again to locate the deer blind and check it out. He crawled through the fence and resumed down the trail. He came to the place where he'd been turning into the deep woods. He'd taken this route every time; it's the one Repeat picked. It approached the clearing for the northwest. He decided to approach the clearing from the north, the side where the deer blind was located. Instead of turning into the deep woods as usual he continued on down the creek for another two hundred yards and then entered the woods.

He took the brass compass and looked at it. When facing the woods, north was directly behind him.

"Okay," he said, "wherever I am in this part of the woods; to get back here all I have to do is walk toward the north. This creek is a good marker," he said, looking around at the slow moving water. Steven began making his way directly south to the clearing. With no trail, the going was slow. He made several detours around thick underbrush and low hanging limbs. He came to a dead log lying across his way. Above it there was a low hanging limb about three inches around. He reached up and grasped the limb, then picked up his feet and legs and swung across the old rotten log and landed on the other side. His right foot hit the dead log causing it to roll over. He didn't notice that about eight feet away, inside the log, was a huge honey bee colony busy about tending their nest and servicing their queen. The buzzing of the creatures increased until it was a roar. Thousands of angry bees formed a swarm, growing larger and larger.

Steven quickly pulled the device out of his pocket and began backing away, watching the angry swarm. Suddenly, the bees attacked. Steven pushed the button, held it down, and repeatedly swept the swarm back and forth. He tripped and fell backward on the ground. Thousands of sleeping bees rained down on him like a carpet. He put his left arm over his face. When the buzzing stopped, he slowly moved his arm. There were two inches of fuzzy insects covering him from the waist up. He sat up. "Boy that was close."

He brushed the bees off himself, got to his feet, and checked his clothes for any that had fallen inside his shirt. Satisfied, he stepped away from the dead log about twenty yards, then turned and aimed the device, then pushed the button. The swarm rose up, almost as a single entity, then circled their hive, and began to settle down.

"I've got to say on my toes," Steven said to himself, "that could have been bad."

Steven saw the clearing ahead. He stopped and began searching the tops of the trees. He couldn't see anything. "Boy, it must be well hidden," he said quietly.

He proceeded to the clearing and located the deer feeder. It was near the center of the clearing. He went down almost even with it, then took seven large steps into the woods. Walking along the wood line, searching the tee tops, he spotted it. He could just make out a wooden cube about eight feet square. It had a slanted roof and a window on the side nearest the clearing. He made his way over to the tree. It was a larger one, about a foot and a half in diameter. Three pieces of wood about six inches long and two inches thick and four inches high had been nailed to the side of the tree to step on and climb to the first limb. From then on to about twenty feet high there were plenty of limbs on the older tree. Steven started climbing. Minutes later he pulled himself into the deer blind. There was a bench on two sides of the structure and then a short one, about two feet long placed by the window. He tried to picture his dad sitting on that bench, at twelve years old, holding a rifle out the window taking aim at a buck deer.

Steven's mind came back to the moment and to his purpose. His eyes darted around the floor of the deer blind. At first he didn't see anything. Then a dull copper colored piece of metal caught his eye. He got on his knees and fished it out of the crack right at the wall. It was an empty shell, but, it wasn't crimped. This one was a real bullet. It popped into his mind that somebody had actually shot Repeat for real. Anger swept his face. Then he realized something. The shell was tarnished and dirty. It had been here a long time. The weather had done its thing, as it does with all things that are left subject to its influence.

"This," Steven said, looking at the spent shell, "is a leftover from last deer season." He breathed a sigh of relief and resumed his search. Looking along the cracks of the make-shift floor, systematically checking every dead leaf and clod of dirt that many pairs of hunting boots had brought up this tree, he spotted a bright tube sticking from under a dead leaf.

"Oh, my God!" he exclaimed hurriedly raking the pieces of the tree leaf from over the object. He used the empty shell to pry the shiny cartridge out of the crack in the floor. It was crimped!

"Ahhhhhhhh," Steven shouted holding it up in front of his face. "Somebody did shoot Repeat with a tranquilizer rifle. Repeat's still alive!" Steven stepped over to the window of the blind and surveyed the clearing. He noticed that the bush where he found the device was right in the center of the window, when you were sitting on the short bench.

"Repeat did go back to that bush," Steven said. "I'll bet he sniffed all around it again and that's when he got shot."

Steven quickly climbed down the tree, jumping from the bottom limb. He ringed the tree to see if he could find a man's footprints. He had obliterated any prints next to the tree with his own. He moved out about five or six feet and searched the ground. There they were, headed straight for the bush in the clearing. They were faint so Steven had to take his time to not lose the trail. It took him about ten minutes to pick out each track and follow them. When they reached the bush, there was side by side prints, then the trail continued across the clearing toward the south. They were more distinct, easier to follow.

"He picked up Repeat; the added weight!" Steven shouted, then grabbed his mouth.

"I've got to calm down," he thought, *"I don't want this guy to hear me before I see him."* Steven continued following the trail deeper and deeper into the woods. Soon, he realized he was getting far away from the clearing and still further from Grandma's house. He was now deep in the woods he had not been in and did not know. He took the device out of his pocket and kept it in his hand. He felt safer just having it ready.

A quarter-mile farther on he came to a log lying across the path of the tracks he was following. He noticed the footprints were side by side again.

"He sat down here to rest," Steven said. "Repeat's getting heavy." Steven stepped over the log and quickened his step. He walked the trail as fast as he could without losing it. When he missed a footprint on grass or leaves, he'd go back and double check until he was sure he was still following the same trail. Thirty minutes later the trail stopped again at a tree stump. By now this guy had carried Repeat as least a mile and a half. Steven sat down in the stump himself and rested for a few minutes then continued his vigil; following the tracks of someone that had his friend. He gripped the device for reassurance then marched on. Twenty minutes later, he slowly became aware of a faint sound, repeating over and over. He held his breath and listened intently. He recognized the bark.

"That's Repeat!" he shouted. He cupped his hand around his mouth and shouted at the top of his voice, then again. The repeated barks never changed.

"He can't hear me," Steven said, "I'm not loud enough." He resumed the trail hurrying as fast as he could keep following the tracks. Minutes later he topped a hill and in the distance he saw a cleared-out area, a mobile home, two vehicles, a flatbed truck and a black car. There was a pen with high sides made with chicken wire. He could just make out movement inside the pen. Steven made his way around the clearing, staying just inside the wooded area. Rounding a clump of bushes, he saw the pen. There was a guy, wearing a funny suit with thick pads all over it, hitting Repeat with a stick. Repeat was fighting him, biting the padded suit and growling. Steven took a breath. "Hey!"

The man in the pen stopped hitting Repeat and turned toward Steven. Repeat, holding onto the thick training suit was swung, body and all, around behind the man.

"Who are..." Steven leveled the device and dropped him. Repeat was still growling and dragging the suited trainer.

"Repeat!" Steven yelled. Repeat's head snapped up. He saw Steven and ran toward him, trying to climb the high wire of the training pen.

"I don't like to have to do this, boy, but it's necessary." Steven pointed the device and put his friend to sleep. He hurriedly located the gate to the pen, went in and picked up Repeat and then turned to the sleeping trainer.

"I'll be back to wake you up even though you don't deserve it. It's not for you; it's for me." Steven carried Repeat well into the woods back toward home. He laid him down gently on a grassy area then rubbed his head several times.

"Good to see you, Repeat. I'll be back soon and wake you up, and then we're going home."

Steven made his way back to the clearing and the mobile home, and then, again, worked his way around to the side, concealing himself just in case someone else was home and just happen to come outside. Steven didn't want to have to put any more people to sleep. This rescue was already complicated enough. He could wake up this guy from the tree line and then just go get Repeat and go home. Steven rounded the bushes and pulled out the device. He leaned around the bushes, device in hand, and looked in the pen.

It was empty! The sleeping dog trainer was gone. Someone must have come out and found him. Steven glanced toward the vehicles. The truck was still there but the black car was gone. No doubt, they rushed him to the hospital, maybe thinking he had a heart attack or something. The rescue of Repeat had just gotten a lot more complicated. He had to wake up the dog trainer, bad guy or not. He was mean to dogs; but he didn't deserve to sleep until he died. He would have to find out where the guy was, probably the hospital, then figure out how to get in his room and wake him up.

Right now, he would go wake up his friend and take him home. Repeat did deserve that.

Steven hurried back to Repeat. When he was within twenty feet, he pushed the button and woke up his sleeping friend. Repeat hopped up, barked, then looked around and spotted Steven. He ran and jumped from six feet away into his arms. Steven hugged him several times. Repeat kept trying to lick his face. Steven let him a couple of times then hugged him down.

"Let's go home, boy," he said, then pulled out his compass and looked at the needle to verify the right direction. Repeat started trotting north, when he got up ahead, he paused and waited for Steven.

"You know the way home, don't you, boy," Steven said and put the compass back in his pocket.

Steven crawled through the fence at the edge of the farm; Repeat ducked under and continued toward home. Steven, walking up the creek toward his bridge, spotted Grandma and Grandpa standing on high ground by the corral scanning the farm.

"Oh," Steven said under his breath, "it's after lunch. They are probably worried are looking for me." Repeat spotted Grandpa, barked that loud, penetrating bark and started running toward him. Steven waved, grinning. Grandpa picked up Repeat and hugged him. Repeat barked loudly again. Grandpa smiled and hugged him again. Repeat got a free one. Grandma petted Repeat then turned to Steven as he caught up with Repeat.

"You found him!" Grandma said. "Where was he?"

Steven knew he could not tell them the whole truth, not yet. He turned and pointed toward the part of the woods where the clearing was located.

"I went well into the deep woods on the hunch that if Repeat was lost, I might get lucky and hear him since he's so loud. Dad gave me a compass so I could find my way back. When I was a couple of miles into the woods, I did hear him. It was very faint, but I distinctly heard his bark. I followed the sound and came upon a home which had a big dog pen in the back and Repeat was in there with a bunch of other dogs," Steven fibbed. "I went to the door but nobody was home, so I went and got Repeat and brought him home. I figured these people happened to see Repeat out in the woods and thought that he was a stray or lost and took him home, put him in their pen and fed him."

"That simply," Grandpa said. "We would have never known if you hadn't gotten interested and come down here to find him."

"I knew that something had happened, Grandpa. Me and Repeat are best friends.

"I know," Grandpa said.

Steven called his mother and told her the good news, relating his truth based, but slightly altered, story. Congratulations came pouring through the phone from his parents. A miracle had happened. They praised Steven for his steadfastness and vigil on behalf of his friend, Repeat. He told them that he wanted to spend perhaps a day or so with Repeat then he'd be home.

Steven decided he would wait to talk to them about bringing Repeat to Dallas. Something else was more important right now.

Chapter 18

TRANSFERED

Sheriff Sheldon Biggs hung up the phone. He turned to his assistant: "Sarah, I've got a name I want you to run through the computer; a Merle Finch, around forty years old; that would put his date of birth around 1970." Sarah nodded and turned to her computer terminal. Her fingers flowed smoothly over the keyboard. A moment later she looked at the sheriff.

"Got a hit. It seems that Mr. Finch has been a bad boy." She printed a copy of the report and handed it to the sheriff. He studied the printout for a few moments.

"Illegal dog fighting," he read. "I hate people that abuse helpless animals; especially man's best friend. Says here he's wanted in Dallas County. Get them on the phone for me." Moments later Sarah announced: "Dallas DA on the phone, Sheriff."

"Marvin," Sheriff Biggs said, "I just got a call from the hospital here in Clarksville. They just admitted a fella's whose unconscious. He was wearing a special protective suit that dog trainers use to train guard dogs. His cousin,

Buford Thompson, one of our locals, brought him in. The hospital staff said that the cousin was acting very suspicious so they called me. We ran his name and it seems you might be interested in this guy; a Merle Finch." There was a minute or two pause on the line.

"Yeah, we want him. We busted a dog fighting ring; but this guy got away. We've been looking for him for a while. You say he's unconscious?"

"Yeah," the sheriff said, "they don't know why, yet. They said he seems to be just sleeping, but they can't wake him up. The cousin said he was training a dog behind his place. The cousin went out there and found this character out cold."

"Maybe he's faking. Maybe he woke up and saw where he was and decided to pretend he's seriously injured."

"Don't think so, Marvin," Sheriff Biggs replied. "The doc told me he tried a pin prick on the bottom of his foot. Nothing at all. Now, I tell you, anybody would flinch, especially when you don't see it coming."

"Okay," the Dallas County DA said, "we'll take him as is. Can you arrange his transport to County Hospital here in Dallas? I'll post a guard on his room until the guy wakes up. Then we'll address his problem."

"I can do that; first thing in the morning."

"Okay, Sheldon. Thanks for the heads-up on this guy, we've been looking for him for a while."

Steven got into bed in the guest room. His mind was racing along on his new problem. Steven had put a bad guy to sleep to rescue his friend and now, because of some really bad luck, the bad guy had gone missing, still asleep. The problem; the bad guy will never wake up until Steven wakes him up. Steven has the only answer that will wake up the sleeping victim. The doctors will find a way to feed him so he won't starve, but they will never be able to figure out why he's sleeping and not waking up. Steven must wake up the animal trainer, and soon.

He wondered how he could get to the hospital, find out what room the guy is in, then get in there and awaken him. All he needed was one second, just one second, and the problem is solved. He would ask Grandpa to take him to the hospital in the morning. He needed to figure out what to say to Grandpa. Asking Grandma would not work. She would have lots of questions that Steven could not answer. No, Grandpa is the best chance. He would talk to him in the morning. The scene outside slowly turned to blackness. The tree frogs, one of the creatures of the night, began their nightly songs. A certain quietness settled over the room as a strange sense of responsibility settled on Steven's shoulders, and a quiet resolve settled in his heart to make things right.

"What do I say at the hospital to find him?" he mumbled then drifted off to sleep thinking about the problem he must face the next morning. He must wake up a sleeping kidnapper.

Steven, dressed and ready to face his new challenge, sat on the side of his bed, momentarily looking out at the predawn sky. Today he must find a way to get to the dog trainer and wake him up. He had now been sleeping since early yesterday afternoon. No food, no water, just peaceful sleep. The hospital would put him on an I.V., so he would be okay for a while. They could even feed him. But, the longer he was in that state of sleep, a sleep that the doctors could not fix, the more noticeable it would become.

Steven, deep in thought, went into the living room and headed for the kitchen to see if Grandma and Grandpa were up yet. When he was about to turn from the hall and enter the dining room he heard the shuffling of feet on the porch. He went to the front door, opened it a little and looked out. Grandpa was sitting on a bench at the end of the porch looking toward the east. Repeat was sitting at the end of the bench, quietly looking toward the east, then up a Grandpa, then back toward the east. Steven leaned out the door and looked in the easterly direction. He didn't see anything. He pushed the door open and stepped out on the porch. Grandpa looked around and spotted him. Repeat got up and trotted around the bench to Steven. Steven petted him on the head.

"Good morning, Steven," Grandpa said. "It's good to have Repeat back at his post."

"Grandpa, what are you doing out here," Steven said, joining Grandpa on the bench.

"I'm waiting for the sun to come up."

"Why?" Steven said, looking toward the east; noticing that light was invading the night and dawn was imminent.

"Well, I figure if the good Lord would bring the sun up for another day, I could do my part and take care of this farm, your grandma and now, Repeat, again." Grandpa's eyes went back to the east. The yellow orb of the sun was now showing among the trees, highlighting the upper limbs of the larger ones.

"Well, that's it," Grandpa said, "looks like the show's on." Steven glanced at the rising sun then turned back at his grandfather.

"Grandpa, I need to talk to you," he said in a strained voice. Grandpa turned and looked at Steven for a moment then put his left arm around him and hugged him. Much of the tension drained out of him. Grandpa smiled a gentle smile and waited. Steven was quiet for a minute; he didn't want his voice to break when he asked Grandpa a serious question. The question to get the help he needed.

"Are you alright," Grandpa asked. Steven nodded then in a rush of words: "Grandpa, I need for you to take me to town to the hospital, no questions asked." He was looking at his grandfather's face, breathing through an open mouth, waiting for his answer.

Grandpa was silent for a moment. He petted Repeat on the head.

"That request has to do with finding this dog, doesn't it?" Steven didn't respond. He held Grandpa's eyes and remained quiet. Grandpa looked toward the sun again, then at the ground, then back to Steven's face.

"Okay, I'll take you, but I have to ask you two questions." Steven nodded breathing heavily in anticipation.

"Are you hurt?"

"No, Sir."

"Did you hurt somebody rescuing this dog?"

"Well, I didn't really hurt him...."

"Are you going to the hospital to hurt him?"

"No, I'm going to help him." Grandpa nodded. "Let me talk to your grandma and, after chores, we'll go."

"Don't tell Grandma," Steven said hurriedly. Grandpa smiled and held up his hand. "Trust me."

Steven and Grandpa, carrying the two pails of milk to the house and the refrigerator as usual, stopped to open the corral gate. Grandpa cleared his throat.

"Grandma's going with us to town." Steven looked at Grandpa anxiously. He continued. "I told her I was going to take you to the video parlor for a while. She wants to ride along and do some shopping at 'Notions'."

"Notions?" Steven said.

"It's a ladies store; a woman's store; sewing stuff. She's never shopped in that store less than an hour. She'll be there for two or three hours if you don't go get her. I always walk over to the feed store and visit until she's finished. I'll drop you off at the video parlor. You can walk over to the hospital after we leave; it's a couple of blocks behind it. When you finish then walk back to the video parlor. When Grandma's finished we'll pick you up.

"Okay," Steven said.

"How long will it take you at the hospital?"

"One second, ah, I mean just a few minutes."

"Okay," Grandpa said, smiling at Steven, "we have a plan."

Steven walked into the video parlor to the noise of multiple video games running at the same time. He heard laser bursts, Star Wars one liners, and multiple sounds of crashes and the victorious sounds of a direct hit. He walked along the line of machines until he reached a side door. Out on the side street he hurried the two blocks to the small hospital.

The double doors at the entrance were ancient wooden doors with a large pane of glass in the center. Antique brass handles were mated on the two doors. Steven reached up and grasped the handle of the right hand door and pulled. The door was heavy. Getting it open he stepped inside and looked around. To the left, against the wall was a small gift shop with an array of flowers, novelty items, T-shirts, and candies. An older lady was sitting behind a counter working with a bouquet of flowers. She looked up when Steven entered the lobby.

To the right was a large L-shaped desk with an assortment of papers spread out on it. There was a computer on the opposite end of it. There was a woman about as old as his mom sitting behind the desk writing on one of the papers. Across the lobby were three doors spaced about 6 feet apart. There were two large, floor-to-ceiling, mirrors mounted on the walls between the doors.

Steven went over to one of the mirrors then paused looking at his image. "Video game," he whispered. He took the device out of his pocket and started waving it around and stabbing at his image as if Obi-wan, from Star Wars, was in a desperate battle with Darth Vader. The older lady in the gift shop smiled, watching him. The lady behind the desk watched Steven for a moment then cleared her throat. Steven stopped and looked from lady to lady in wide-eyed innocence.

"Sweetheart," she said. "This is a hospital lobby."

"I know," Steven said. "One of my friends said a dog trainer came in here yesterday. I have a dog."

"Honey, you wouldn't want this guy to train your dog, he's a bad person. He hurts dogs. The police are going to arrest him and put him in jail as soon as he gets well. He's on his way right now to County Hospital in Dallas so the doctors there can treat him."

Steven exaggerated a frown. "I won't let him hurt my dog!" Steven said then looked again to the two ladies. "Bye." He went out the doors of the hospital and headed for the video parlor. He went in the side door then walked to the front and looked around the square. He spotted the bus station on the opposite corner. He hurried across the square.

"When does the first bus to Dallas leave in the morning?" The station agent rattled computer keys then looked up. "Ten-fifteen; gets to Dallas at two-twenty-five.

Steven thanked the agent then hurried back to the video store. He saw his grandparents pull up to the store as he was crossing the square. Grandpa entered the video store; Steven entered just behind him. "Grandpa," he called to him. Grandpa turned, "Ah, there you are. Everything okay?"

Steven nodded. "Grandpa, I told Dad that I would be home in a couple of days; tomorrow's the second day. I just checked the bus station and a bus leaves in the morning at ten-fifteen. Can you bring me to the station in the morning?"

"Sure," Grandpa said. "We hate to see you leave so soon."

"I'll be back, often," Steven said. "Things are different now."

"I'm glad," Grandpa said.

Chapter 19

THE QUEST

Back in Dallas, Steven sat in his room wrestling with the problem of getting close enough to Merle Finch to awaken him. He had learned his name from news broadcast about animal abuse. When he had gotten home yesterday afternoon and watched the evening news, a short news item about an unconscious man that had been transferred to Dallas after being apprehended in Northeast Texas. The man in question was wanted for illegal dog fighting activity. The DA had posted a guard at the hospital to await his recovery. Then, Merle Finch would stand trial.

Steven went on the Internet and brought up the bus routes of the city. He needed to get to County Hospital. He noted that the closest bus stop was four blocks from his house. That's okay. He systematically traced the complete route to the hospital. He carefully recorded the information. He checked his wallet. He had enough money left over from the trip to Grandma's house. All set.

Steven looked at his watch. Forty-two minutes until the bus arrived at his first bus stop. He touched his pocket. The device was still there. He went out the door and headed for the bus stop. He walked the four blocks with a brisk step, then sat down on the bench, and looked at his watch. It was still thirty-two minutes until the bus was scheduled to arrive. Steven began to think about how he was going to handle the problems ahead. He had to get this done. This was a mission of mercy. The kidnapper, and abuser, had been stopped. His plan, whatever it was, had been foiled and he was in custody and going to jail, that is, as soon as Steven woke him up.

Getting to the hospital had been worked out; no problem. The next thing would be finding out which room the guy is in—that might be a problem. He'd have to deal with that when he got there. Getting in his room in secret; that might be a problem. There was a policeman guarding the door. Maybe, when he had the room located and got to it, if the coast was clear, he could put the guard to sleep. Once he's asleep he could just open the door of the hospital room, wake the guy up, and close it. Then just be walking by and wake up the guard. That would be easy, if nobody was in the hall. Steven looked at his watch again; eight more minutes.

Several miles away, at County Hospital, a specialist in sleep disorders, the police officer assigned to guard the room, and three other doctors stood in a group in the room of Merle Finch. Police records showed that Merle Finch, thirty-eight years old, had a long record of animal abuse; illegal dog fighting, and illegal gambling. He'd been in jail two times before. The group looked at the patient that had slept now for some forty-three hours in a peaceful deep sleep. His breathing was deep and regular.

"That's the most perfect state of sleep I've ever seen," the specialist said. "His brain's message center is simply turned off. He does not respond to any stimulation. And, gentlemen, I don't know why. He's not in any danger that I can determine."

"Do you think he'll wake up?" the police officer asked.

"I don't know. He could wake up at any time. I don't find any reason why he wouldn't. However," the specialist continued, "I don't know why he hasn't already." The three doctors nodded. The police officer looked at the sleeping man again.

"I wish I could sleep like that, however, I would want to wake up."

The specialist left instructions to keep the patient under observation for the next couple of days while he studied the results of the test and consulted with some of his colleagues.

Steven, sitting on the bench waiting for the first leg of his journey to begin, looked at his watch once more; four more minutes. Then he saw the bus a half-block away steering through the traffic toward the bus stop. When it stopped and the door opened two people got off. Seven got on the bus and paid the driver.

"What time is it," Steven asked. The driver stretched out his arm, looked at his watch. "Sixteen after." Steven looked at his watch, popped the stem and adjusted the time. "Thanks," he said and took a seat up front.

"Where are you going this fine day," the driver asked glancing over his shoulder as he pulled the bus away from the curb.

"To the hospital," Steven answered.

"Oh," The driver said with a sympathetic look on his face. Steven smiled a little without opening his mouth. The driver focused his attention on the traffic. Steven looked out the window. This was his first time to ride a bus in the city that wasn't a school bus. It seemed so quiet, like the greyhound bus he rode to Grandma's. Adults don't talk and stuff on the bus like kids do. He wondered why they quit when they grow up. The adult world…Different. He shifted himself in the seat. This was something very important that he was doing. He pulled out his notes and studied them again. Each time the bus stopped he would check the street to see if it was his stop. At the next stop he had a forty-five-minute wait for the right bus to go close to County Hospital. The fourth stop he saw it and got off the bus.

Steven watched the bus pull away and then he sat down on the bench. He looked around at the intersection. Cars would pile up when the light was red, then go when the light turned green. He watched the array of changing automobiles and the people in them. A station wagon stopped right in front of him. A young girl, his age, looked out the window of the back seat and smiled at him. Steven smiled back, then watched the car drive away when the light changed.

When the street was clear again, his eyes went up. Across the street was a high school. Four guys were jogging around a playing field. They were lean and muscular. Steven looked down at his bicep, then flexed it. It barely stood up. He looked at the high school guys again.

"You don't have to have big muscles," he thought. He glanced at his watch; forty-one more minutes. He stood, looked around again, then walked back and forth a few times, then

looked at his watch again. Thirty-nine more minutes.

"Boy, it seems like a long time," he muttered, then sat back down and looked down the street.

"Hi there, young man." Steven jumped, jerked around, and caught his breath. An old man had walked up and sat down on the bench so quietly that he hadn't heard him. He had a cane standing on the ground in front of him and had both wrinkled hands on it. He smiled when Steven looked at him. "Sorry, I didn't mean to scare you."

"It's okay," Steven said. "I didn't hear you come up and sit down." The old man nodded and smiled. He was silent for a moment, then he looked over at Steven. "Young man, you seem a little up tight like something's bothering you. You okay?" the old man asked in a voice mellowed and softened with age. Steven looked at the old man's face. He found himself relaxing at the sound of his voice. He felt a rush of words come up to his chest, opened his mouth, and closed it again. He couldn't just start talking about his mission to a stranger. Not to anybody. "I'm okay," He said. "Why do you think I'm uptight?"

"You're sitting there like you could jump ten feet in any direction if necessary." Steven couldn't help but smile. He sat back on the bench, crossed him arms, and looked at his watch. Twenty-four more minutes.

"You going to the hospital?" the old man asked.

"Yeah," Steven said.

"Me, too. Name's Oliver Thurman," he said, extending his hand. Steven took it. "Steven...Steven Krebs," he said, shaking Oliver's hand. Oliver placed his hand back on top of the one on his cane.

"You go by Stevie?"

"I used too, but I like Steven better."

"Steven it is," Oliver said, smiling. "Call me Oliver. Wilma, my wife, is in the hospital for a few days. She fell and bruised her hip." Steven nodded and then looked at his watch again. The old man noticed Steven checking his watch, reached inside his suit coat and pulled out a two-inch diameter, half-inch thick, gold, Hamilton Railroad Watch and looked at it. Steven stared at the watch. Oliver noticed his interest in the antique chronometer and opened his hand and extended the time piece toward Steven. He looked at Oliver, then picked up the pocket watch.

"My father gave that to me forty-five years ago. He was a railroad conductor."

"Wow, it's heavy," Steven said. He looked at the face of the watch, at the white background with black numerals and spear looking hands, black also. There was a secondary dial the size of a dime below the big hands. A tiny black hair-sized hand was marking the seconds. The early century pocket watch was beautiful.

"How much did it cost?" Steven said.

"My father gave three hundred dollars for it in nineteen hundred and twenty-five. Now, it's priceless. I'm passing it on to my grandson; he's twelve now." Steven put his wristwatch beside it and compared the times. The two chronometers were exactly together. The railroad watch dwarfed his silver colored wristwatch with its imitation leather band. Steven handed the watch back to Oliver.

"It's really beautiful."

The bus drove up and stopped just as Oliver was putting the watch back in his inside coat pocket. He leaned forward to stand; Steven put his hand on his elbow and assisted him. Oliver, on his feet, looked at Steven and smiled. They boarded the bus. Just as the driver was closing the door two shady looking characters came running toward the bus. One of them shouted for the driver to wait. The driver pushed the door back open and the two men got on the bus. One of them was wearing a gray T-shirt that had the sleeves torn out of it. The other had on a checkered shirt and wore it with the shirt tail out. Both of them had tattoos of a snake on their left forearms.

Steven had not noticed that the two had been standing near the bus stop and observing Oliver displaying the valuable gold watch.

Oliver sat down on the front seat of the bus. Steven took the second seat across the aisle. The two characters went to the back of the bus.

Steven began checking the streets at each bus stop. Each time the bus stopped more people got on. When they arrived at the bus stop a half a block from County Hospital the bus was full of people. Steven was the third person off the bus. Oliver was first, then a lady, then Steven. He stepped from the sidewalk onto the grass and looked toward the hospital. The complex was huge. Now he had to locate the right building, go in, and figure out how to find the sleeping trainer's room, then sneak in and wake him up.

While Steven was deep in thought, the people filed off the bus and walked away in different directions. He glanced around to try to locate Oliver. He saw him walking slowly about a half a block from the bus stop. He was going the wrong way, away from the hospital. Steven frowned. The two shady characters were the last two to get off the bus. They turned immediately and started walking at a fast pace toward Oliver. The bus pulled away, passing the two, as they hurried along the sidewalk. Steven watched them for a moment then looked at the ground. When he looked back up, the character wearing the gray T-shirt was holding Oliver from the back. The other guy had his hand inside the old man's coat. The guy let go of Oliver and the two men started running across the grass toward some buildings. Steven pulled out the device.

"They're some distance away," he muttered. Steven ran twenty yards in their direction then leveled the device and pushed the button. The two characters went down on the grass. Steven turned and ran to Oliver. He was down on one knee and leaning on his cane. Steven helped him up. He looked confused and frightened.

"You okay?" Steven said.

"My watch!" Oliver responded; "they took my watch."

"I'll get it," Steven said. "You wait right here and I'll get it for you." Oliver steadied himself on his cane and watched Steven run across the grass toward the two men lying on the ground. Steven approached the two characters, felt their pockets and located the watch, retrieved it and hurried back to Oliver. He placed the precious time piece in Oliver's hand and smiled. Oliver looked at it, held it to his ear for a moment, satisfied, he put it in his pocket and patted his coat. He looked at the two men lying on the grass sound asleep then back at Steven.

"How did you do that?"

"Don't ask, okay," Steven said. Oliver studied Stevens' face for a moment, then looked at the two men, still sleeping, then back to Steven's eyes.

"Thank you," he said.

"You're welcome, Sir. Why were you walking this way, away from the hospital?"

"There's a little flower shop in the next block. I always take Wilma a rose."

"Oh, I'll walk with you," Steven said. "I'd like to ask you some questions if it's okay."

"Sure," Oliver responded. "Thank you again for getting my watch back."

They started for the little flower shop Oliver frequented during his wife's stay in the hospital. The curving sidewalk took them closer to the two sleeping men. Steven carefully lagged behind momentarily, took out the device, and awakened the two characters. He watched until he saw them set up, then hurried back up beside Oliver. Oliver paused, turned slowly, and looked toward the two men. He saw them sitting up talking to each other. When Steven was beside him again he looked at Steven's face. Steven smiled. Oliver returned the smile. There was intrigue in his eyes. Oliver was quiet for a moment, then he glanced at Steven, then back toward the flower shop.

"What is your question," he said. They entered the flower shop. Oliver purchased a single, long stem rose. The sales lady packaged the rose in a long narrow box and handed it to Oliver. They exited the door and began the walk to the hospital complex.

"Ah, my question," Steven said. "How can I find out what room somebody's in at the hospital?" Oliver, walking along with his cane in one hand and the flower in the other, looked at Steven.

"You mean without asking at the information desk." Steven nodded.

"Do you know this person's name?"

"Merle Finch," Steven said. "His name is Merle Finch." Oliver paused a moment.

"Finch? That's the guy they caught setting up dog fights. I saw it on the news. They'll be a guard on his door." Steven nodded. Oliver stopped and turned to Steven.

"You're not going to hurt that policeman, are you?"

"No, I'm going to help him."

"You're not going to hurt that fella in that room?"

"No, I'm going to help him, too." They came to the place where Oliver was assaulted. Oliver looked toward the grassy area. The men were gone. He looked at Steven. Steven smiled. Oliver nodded.

"I can tell that you are a good boy and wouldn't want to hurt anybody. Since there's a policeman guarding the room, all you need to know is what floor he's on. When you see the policeman that will be the room. I'll find out what floor he's on."

"How?" Steven said.

"Trust me," Oliver said. "Sometimes being old is kinda' cool. If they get suspicious I'll act senile. When you're eighty-two you can get away with a lot." Oliver grinned, enjoying the intrigue and the adventure. Steven smiled. He liked his new acquaintance, he was good and he was going to help.

Steven and Oliver entered the hospital. The coolness of the air conditioning bathed their faces when the automatic doors opened. Oliver immediately turned to the right, went over to a waiting area, and sat down. Steven followed and sat down beside him.

"I need to sit here for just a moment," Oliver said.

"It's okay," Steven said. Oliver leaned back in the chair, crossed his legs, and put his cane between his toes, holding it with both hands. He leaned toward Steven and spoke quietly: "Is there anything I should know about this guy before I make my move? How did you get involved with him?"

"He abused my dog," Steven said. "I'm going to help him because he still doesn't deserve to be punished forever. The law's going to deal with him."

"Okay," Oliver said, getting up. "Stand behind me and look blank."

"Blank?"

"Like a nerd," Oliver said and smiled.

"Oh," Steven said. "No problem." Oliver approached the information desk, Steven in tow. The middle-aged lady looked up at him, at Steven, then back to Oliver.

"May I help you?" Oliver held up his cane so the lady could see it.

"What room is Merle Finch in?" Oliver said. Steven heard the clicking of computer keys. The lady studied the computer screen for a moment, then looked at Oliver.

"Are you a relative, Sir?" she said guardedly.

"No, but my wife's in this hospital," Oliver said in a concerned voice.

"Her name is?..." the lady inquired.

"Wilma Thurman." Steven heard the keys again.

"She'll be just fine, Sir. Your wife is on the second floor, room 225. Mr. Finch is in 312 on the third floor. Besides, there's a policeman guarding him. Also, they're moving him to another building today, to a psychiatric ward. There will be no problem."

"Thank you," Oliver said. "You're a nice young lady." The lady smiled sweetly and pushed her hair back.

"Come along, Son," Oliver said and went to the elevator. Steven followed.

Chapter 20

THE ROSE

The elevator stopped on the second floor and the door glided open. Oliver stepped out onto the second floor then turned to face Steven. Steven reached and secured the door when it began closing. Oliver studied him for a moment, then nodded perceptibly.

"Good luck and thanks again."

"You're welcome, Oliver, and I'm glad I met you."

"Me, too. If you get cornered upstairs, you have a friend in room 225."

"Thank you, Sir." Oliver nodded, then turned, readjusted the box containing the rose under his arm, and headed down the hall to room 225. Steven watched him walk momentarily; there was *something* about the way he carried the box with the single rose inside.

Steven released the door and pushed the button for the third floor again. When the elevator resumed, he laid his hand on his pocket to feel the device. The elevator eased to a stop and the door opened. Steven stepped out. He noticed that his heart was pounding and he was breathing with his mouth open. He closed it, took a deep breath and exhaled, then took another.

"I've got to remember to look cool and relaxed," he reminded himself softly. He looked around. To his left was a long hallway. He could see four doors on each side. At the end of the hall there was a big picture of a nurse in an old-timey uniform. He could barely make it out. A hallway went to the left and another to the right from the big picture. Steven looked the other way down the hall. On the right there was some glass doors that looked like offices. On the left there was a storage room. Then, passed that was the nurses' station. He saw two nurses sitting at a long desk working with records and a nurse and a doctor standing in the hall next to the nurses' station looking at a clipboard. So far, they hadn't paid any attention to Steven's presence in the hallway.

Steven turned to the left and preceded along the hallway. He checked the number on the first door on the right; 338. The next door on the left was 339. He stopped; room 312, Merle Finch, was the other way, past the nurses' station. He was going to have to walk past the station. So far, no one had paid any attention to him. However, when he walks by they are going to notice him and probably ask him if they could help him. What could he say?

He thought for a minute. Nothing. If he said he wanted to see Merle Finch, they would want to know who he was and would notify the policeman on the door. That won't work.

Steven, facing the empty hallway, glanced over his shoulder. Still no one had noticed him. He started walking toward the big picture, thinking. Suddenly, he stopped, looked at the floor for a moment, then turned and hurried back to the elevator, entered, and pushed the button for the second floor. When the doors opened, he stepped out, turned to the left and hurried along, checking the doors for room 225.

The door was open. He walked up to the door and looked in. There was a gray haired old lady lying in the hospital bed leaning up against the head of the bed on two pillows. Oliver, his friend, was sitting beside the bed in a chair holding her hand. In her other hand was the long stem red rose. When Steven appeared at the door, Oliver looked around and smiled.

"Steven, come in," he said cordially, then turned to Wilma: "This is the young man I was telling you about."

"Oh, he's such a handsome young man," Wilma said, "and so brave." The gray haired old lady's eyes sparkled. Steven smiled and shrugged awkwardly. Oliver looked at him again. "Everything okay?"

"Yeah," Steven said. "I was just wondering if I could borrow your red rose for a minute. I'll bring it right back, I promise." Wilma looked at the rose, then at Oliver, and back to Steven. "Why?" she said. Oliver looked at Steven then turned to Wilma. "Don't ask, okay," then gently gripped her hand. Wilma looked over at Oliver and he winked. A smile slowly formed on Wilma's lips. She looked at Steven, smiled, and extended the rose toward him. He reached out and took it. "I'll bring it right back to you," He promised. He glanced at Oliver and left the room.

He hurried back to the elevator, entered, and pushed the button for the third floor. When the elevator starting rising he straightened up. "Now it's time to look like a Nerd," he said out loud. He stepped out of the elevator, turned to the right, and started walking down the hall carrying the rose in front of him. The doctor and the nurse with the clipboard were gone. The two nurses sitting at the desk glanced up, saw Steven, and looked at the rose. They looked at each other and smiled, then focused again on their records keeping. When Steven was well past the nursses' station he started breathing again.

It worked!

Steven began looking for room numbers. He passed two blank doors without knobs, only a curved handle with a place for a key. He came to the end of the hall and turned left. He looked down the long hallway. A nurse entered a room three doors down and closed the door behind her. Four more doors down was a police officer sitting in a chair in front of a room.

"That's it," Steven said, "that's where he is." Steven thought for a minute. He could walk up to the policeman, put him to sleep, open the guy's door a little, stick the device in the door and wake him up, close the door, wake up the policeman, and just walk away. Steven went over the sequence in his mind. It seemed too easy. Suppose somebody came around the corner just as he put the policeman to sleep. What then?

He paused a moment. He had to complete his mission. It's a chance he would have to take. He took a deep breath, exhaled, and started walking toward the room. There was a noise behind him. Steven stopped and glanced over his shoulder. Two doctors came walking around the corner into the hallway. Behind them there were two stocky guys in white hospital coats rolling a gurney. Steven stepped over to a window and pretended to be looking out at the hospital complex. The four men walked by without even looking at him.

When the police officer saw the doctors and the gurney approaching he got up and opened the door of the sleeping man's room. He and the four men with the gurney went inside. Steven waited. He continued looking out the window and glancing at the room. He caught himself sniffing the rose. He glanced around, the hallway was still empty.

A few minutes later, the door of the room opened and one of the men in a white coat backed out of the room pulling a gurney. Steven saw the sleeping Merle Finch lying on it. The second stocky man appeared pushing on the gurney, then the doctors, followed by the policeman. They came down the hall toward Steven. Steven smiled.

What a break! He rotated the device in his pocket and got ready. Just when the gurney was even with him he pushed the button. The awakened Merle Finch suddenly sat up on the gurney and shouted at the top of his voice:

"Who are you?" The man in front of the gurney ran backwards and fell on his back in the middle of the hallway. Merle Finch watched the stocky man in a white coat drop out of his sight. He looked over at the two doctors dressed in white, then around at the other stocky man in his white coat. The police officer, out of Finch's sight pulled out a two-way radio and began speaking into it. Merle Finch could not see anyone's mouth moving. The fallen man got up from the floor. His mouth wasn't moving. Panic formed on the trainer's face.

"What happened," he shouted. "Where am I?" Everyone ignored him. He looked around and saw Steven standing at the window, holding the rose. Steven smiled, sniffed the rose, and winked at Merle Finch. Finch's eyes widened.

"Am I dead, am I dead?" he shouted frantically.

"No, man, you're not dead," the stocky man said, "but you nearly gave me a heart attack." Steven turned toward the window and gritted his teeth to keep from laughing.

"Can I have him, doc?" the policeman said, looking a Merle Finch. The doctor pulled a pencil-sized flashlight from his breast pocket and looked into Finch's eyes, then listened to his heart for a moment. "He's all yours."

The police officer handcuffed the trainer, stated his rights, and helped him off the gurney. When Finch stood up, he stretched, took a deep breath, and looked at the policeman. "I'm hungry."

The policeman locked eyes with him. "I'll bet you are; you've slept for days. Don't worry; where you are going there's three squares a day."

The two doctors went around the corner, stopping at the nurses' station, standing in the hall. The two guys with the gurney rolled it on down the hall. The police officer walked Finch down the hall past the nurses' station and to the elevator. Steven followed carrying the rose in front of him. The two nurses watched the parade, looked at each other and shrugged their shoulders and returned to their duty. Steven waited for the elevator to close with the officer and his prisoner. Then he pushed the button and waited. When it arrived he entered and pushed the button for the second floor.

Sitting at the bus stop, waiting for the first bus on his journey home, Steven's mind began weighing his new world. He had just averted a crisis; a crisis that could have been really bad. It is a serious device. From now on he would use it only in an emergency or something so serious that he simply had too.

He'd been out of school for the summer almost two months now. School would be starting in one more month and he hadn't spent any time with his friends this summer. That is, except for his birthday party. He would call them all and have a meeting about what to do the rest of the summer before school. Perhaps they should not know about the device. Not yet. It was still new to him. He had found out a lot about it. He made a mental list.

1. The sleep was instant.
2. The sleep was permanent until reversed by the device.
3. The sleep caused no problems
4. It did not work in water.
5. It had a limited range

Steven saw the park passing by the window on the left side of the bus, the driver steered into the bus stop and opened the door. Steven stepped off the bus and began the four block walk home. He'd be glad to get there; he was hungry.

Chapter 21

THE BULLY

The first day of school. Steven was excited. He was in the 8th grade. This year was going to be great. As he walked the five blocks to school, twice he placed his hand on his pocket to feel the device. It was there.

He bounded up the entrance steps to the school and pushed the twin doors open and entered the hall. Twenty yards down the hall one of the bullies, Bruce Johnson, had two his Pentium Class friends by the neck, one in each hand, shaking them like rag dolls. He was sneering and the students around him were laughing. Bruce pushed Steven's friends toward the wall. They staggered over and leaned on it.

Anger twisted Steven Krebs face.

He reached into his pocket, rotated the device, pointed it and pushed the button. The bully collapsed instantly, falling face forward onto the hardwood floor. Blood poured from his mouth and nose forming a puddle on the floor. Two girls screamed.

Students came running from up and down the hall. Teachers stuck their heads out the doors of the classrooms then hurried toward the scene.

Steven panicked, pointed the device, and pushed the button again. An awakened Bruce Johnson moaned, his mouth blowing bubbles in the pool of blood. Steven dropped his books, ran out the door, and all five blocks home. The last fifty yards the siren of the passing ambulance burned in his ears.

Rushing in the door of his house, gasping for breath, crying, coughing, unable to speak, he ran up to his mother and pointed toward the school. Panic swept Rhonda Krebs face.

"Steven, what is it!" she exclaimed. Getting no answer, she quickly looked his body over; finding nothing, she grabbed the phone and dialed his father's office. Steven heard her talk rapidly into it and then hang it up.

Soon, Steven's father had his hands on his shoulders.

"What's wrong, Son," he said. Steven was still heaving and crying trying to form words; he didn't know what to say. His father pulled him into his arms. Steven responded by circling his father with his arms and clinging to him.

"It's alright, Son," he heard his father saying, "calm down, it's okay, you can talk to me about anything."

"Can we go to my room," Steven whimpered. His father, holding him in his arms, looked up at his mother; she nodded. His father walked him down the hall, into his room, and closed the door.

Chapter 22

TRUE FRIEND

Steven, his face wet with tears, sniffed his runny nose, and looked at the floor. "I don't know where to start, Dad."

"That's okay, Son. Just start anywhere." Steven looked up at his father's face. It was kind; the face of a friend, like he'd never seen it before.

He began with the incident at school, then started talking about Repeat and finding the device. He took it out of his pocket and handed it to his father. As Steven began talking about it, he got his voice back, and was soon relating the whole story. His father looked at him with gentle eyes, nodding from time to time. When Steven finished, he looked up at his father, holding his breath, not knowing what to expect.

His father handed the device back to him. "Here, Son, put this in your pocket."

Steven's eyes widened as he took the device and complied. His father stood, put his arm around Steven, and walked him back down the hall and into the living room. His mother searched his face and hugged him.

"Steven and I are going to Aurora," his father said. His parents locked eyes for a moment, then his mother nodded.

"Why?" Steven said.

"It's important," he father answered.

During the three-hour drive to Aurora Steven's father asked him questions, sparking his desire to relive the entire adventure. Smiling and nodding when Steven would make a point, chuckling at the adventures of Repeat, and laughing out loud at the purse snatcher's mid-stride snooze.

When Steven went over the adventure of Repeat's rescue, the whole truth this time, his dad listened intently. When Steven finished, his dad glanced at him and then back at the road ahead. "I knew there was something special going on for you to give the fact of Repeat's disappearance so much importance. I thought maybe it was something like Repeat saving your life or rescuing you somehow or the other way around. You did rescue Repeat; and not only that, you rescued the bad guy from serious trouble that would, apparently, eventually lead to his death.

Steven liked his dad; he was cool; you could talk to him. He wondered why they were going to Aurora. Steven knew that his mom and dad inherited some property there from his dad's parents. But that was a long time ago.

His father drove the car up into the yard of an old farmhouse. The house looked like it hadn't been lived in for a long time. The yard was overgrown with grass and weeds. The door of the old house was standing half way open on a porch with some of the boards missing. His dad reached over and got a flashlight out of the glovebox, got out of the car, and waved for Steven to follow. They proceeded across the yard and into the house.

"Son, watch your step, some of the floor boards may be rotted out." His dad went into the back room of the abandoned structure and opened a closet. The door scrapped the floor while he forced it open. Inside the closet there was a trap door in the floor. His dad positioned himself and lifted the dusty wooden door and pushed it all the way open, propping it against the side wall. He shined the light down a flight of stairs. Steven counted seven steps. His dad held the side rail and went slowly down the stairs to the bottom then waited for Steven. Steven, enjoying the intrigue, walked down the stairs.

His dad went straight to the back wall to the right hand corner. He shined the flashlight on the dark brown bricks of the wall. He started on the second row from the bottom, then counted six bricks from the corner. With his hand on the brick, he handed Steven the flashlight. Steven took it and shined it on the brick. His father started working the brick out of its place in the wall. It was stiff with dust at first but after working it up and down for a moment, it slid out of the wall. Steven eagerly shined the light into the open hole. He saw the reflection of a red metal box. His dad reached inside the hole and grasped the box and slide it out of the opening. It was about the size of a sheet of notebook paper and two inches deep.

His dad turned and set the box down on the floor of the basement and raised the lid. Steven shined the light into the box.

His device!

Steven quickly touched his pocket. He still had it! He pulled it out of his pocket and looked at it. The green light was glowing. He reached down into box and picked up the second one. The green light came on. He held them side by side and looked one to the other. The green lights were glowing brightly in the darkened basement. Steven looked up at his dad.

"You found one, too!"

"When I was twelve. I was playing in the creek bottom. I started home and when I came to the back of the farm I saw a ship sitting on the grass close to the fence. A real skinny man was looking at a cow that was lying on the ground. He had a camera-looking thing, on a tripod, aimed at the cow. While I was watching he pointed that at the cow and the cow got up. The animal's movement knocked over the guy's camera. He quickly gathered up all the stuff he had on the ground, got into his ship and left. I went over there to look at the tracks the ship made and there it was, down in the grass." Steven's dad took a couple of breaths.

"I called it a sleep gun," he continued. I had a lot of fun with it. Animals, insects, birds, crawdads; I guess I put everything on Grandpa's farm asleep two or three times. Then one Saturday I was playing in the school house. The janitor came in on Saturday to clean and wax some of the floors. He jumped on me for playing in the school on Saturday. I got mad and pointed it at him and pushed the button. He fell awkwardly against a banister at the edge of the hall and broke his arm really bad. I saw a bone sticking out and he was bleeding on the floor. I woke him back up then ran to my grandfather and told him that I saw the janitor fall at the school and he was bleeding. Grandpa ran over there to check on him"

Steven's dad paused a moment and composed himself.

"That day, I dug that brick out of the wall and put the *sleep gun* in there."

Steven and his father held each other's eyes for a long moment. Something passed between them that neither had words to express.

Steven's father, carrying the metal box with both remotes inside, ascended the stairs from the basement with Steven following. They went through the living room and out the front door onto the porch. They paused a moment to let their eyes adjust to the bright sunlight. Moments later they stepped off the porch and headed for the car. Suddenly a beam of blue light locked onto the metal box in Donald's hand. Static electricity began to make his fingers tingle. He dropped the box and he and Steven looked up toward the source of the beam of intense light. There was a silvery sphere about thirty feet in diameter hovering a hundred feet above the car. Donald grabbed Steven's arm and pulled him back toward the house well clear of the metal box lying on the ground. A moment later the beam disappeared then the craft rose slowly for a moment and then accelerated into the sky and was gone. Donald and Steven stood in place for a stunned moment. They then looked at each other and then at the metal box lying in the yard in front of the car.

"What was that!?" Steven exclaimed staring into an empty sky.

"I don't know," Donald said. "But I've got a feeling that metal box is now empty or those two devices no longer work." Steven's eyes went to the metal box.

Donald approached it cautiously with Steven walking beside him. They squatted down and studied it. Donald carefully reached down and touched it to see if it was hot. It was very cool to the touch.

"It's cold," Donald said. He opened it. It was empty.

On the way back home Steven's Dad glanced at him. "Well, Son, there's now no reason to report this. There's no evidence. It would just be a story that can't be proven."

"Dad," Steven said, "why didn't they come and get yours a long time ago?"

"The only thing I can think of is the fact that shortly after I found it I buried it underground and they could not detect where it was located. The one you had led them to it."

They rode along the highway for some time in silence; then Donald observed.

"We both had an opportunity to learn something about power and about controlling it. As it turned out, it could be called a test."

"Did we pass?"

"I think so, Son…I think so."

END

ABOUT THE AUTHOR

Dan Holt is a U.S. Army veteran, having served three years as a Communications Specialist in Germany. He spent the remainder of his civilian career as a self-taught engineer, designing and testing large-scale production equipment for the file folder industry. The efficiency and durability of his designs even garnered interest from some foreign manufacturers.

In retirement, Dan has used his writing skills to express his continuing fascination with machinery and science fiction. His zest for adventure and intrigue continue to rule in his three other novels: UNDERNEATH THE MOON, UNDERNEATH THE MOON 2, and KEEPSAKE. His variety in sci-fi thought will be evident in his soon-to-be-released novel, UNDERNEATH THE MOON 3, the last novel in that series

See all of Dan's works at the publisher's web site, www.maxholtmedia.com.